WHO WAS SYLVIA?

- A MAXEY BURNELL MYSTERY -

CAROL CAIL

A Deadly Alibi Press LTD. BOOK

Deadly Alibi Press Ltd.
PO Box 5947
Vancouver, WA 98668-5947

Library of Congress Catalog Card Number: 99-65967

ISBN: 1-886199-04-3 (Acid free trade paper)

“What’s the use of calling the police, Calen? The jerk’s long gone. They can’t do anything.”

“Maxey, the police need to know about this. What if he’s out there terrorizing some other woman right now?”

“No! It was me he wanted. He called me ‘Missy,’ but he also called me by name. He was hiding near the house and he taunted me—’A-a-a-xey.’”

Other Maxey Burnell Mysteries
by Carol Cail

Private Lies
Unsafe Keeping
If Two of Them Are Dead

This one has to be for all my long time
friends at Daily Office Supply.

1

"I'm worried about Sylvia Wellman." Maxey said it loud enough to waken herself and Calen, who was sleeping over.

"Who's Sylvia Wellman?" he mumbled, snugging her closer and hauling the sheet up under their chins.

Maxey, distracted by the surprise of having talked herself awake, murmured, "I have no idea."

Calen rearranged his legs, sinking toward oblivion again.

"That's the problem," Maxey said. Past the point of no return to sleep, she frowned into the dark. "I don't know anything about her except she died yesterday and I had to release her to the mortuary."

Calen grunted. Moe, feeling left out of the early hours' conversation, called cat questions from the other side of the bedroom door.

Maxey resolved to be good and not disturb Calen any more. He'd arrived after she was already in bed, his shoulders sagging from a rough day of monthly reports, and he had some kind of arson seminar to teach in the morning. She stroked the nap of his beard, a carefully trimmed quarter inch all around.

Moe gave up and padded away from the door. A gust of October chinook rattled the south windows. Calen sighed and caught her hand to kiss the palm. "Okay, I've gotta ask. Why did you have to release the body of a complete stranger?"

"Apparently she didn't have any relatives. Or friends even. God, that's sad, isn't it? She was in the hospital because she fell and broke a hip, and she developed pneumonia and she died."

"An old lady, huh?"

"No. She was only sixty-four."

"I thought you didn't know anything about her."

"I don't!"

"Why did the hospital call you?"

"They were checking through her belongings and found one of my business cards. So they phoned me."

Calen yawned in Maxey's ear. "You aren't going to get stuck with her hospital bill, are you?"

"Oh, no, she had insurance, Medicare, or something."

Moe came back to request admittance, his voice louder, testier.

Calen yawned again. "Did you have to go over to Boulder Community to sign the papers?"

"I didn't have to. They faxed them to me. Now I kind of wish I'd gone in person. Viewed the body, maybe. Oh, for gosh sake, Moe!" She threw off the covers and tried to sit up.

"Here. I'll do it." Calen hauled her down again. "Shut up, Moe, or it's generic dry rations for the next three days."

In a sitcom, the cat would have understood this and desisted in mid-rowel. In real life, the cat didn't even hear it and won admittance to the foot of the bed, his fat, warm weight separating Maxey and Calen from the knees down.

The wail woke them a few hours later—fire trucks sirening close by. Calen threw off the blanket, dislodging Moe in the process, and hurried to the window overlooking

Spruce Street. He pulled the blind too hard, and it jumped up and flapped around the roller. Groaning, Maxey scuffed her feet into slippers and tied on her flannel robe and went to look out, too. A flickering glow backlit the houses across the street. Red and blue lights strafed the undersides of the trees. There was the distant but unmistakable sound of breaking glass.

"What's over on the other side of that block? Facing Pearl Street?" Calen asked.

"Several stores. I'm not sure which one would be due south of here. There's a dry cleaner's, an oriental rug place, um, office supply, futon shop. Oh, and a fortune teller."

Calen flexed his knees to raise the window sash. The wind rushed in, bringing the sounds of shouting and the trenchant stink of burning building. He shivered.

Maxey opened her robe and pressed against his bare back, enfolding him as far as the flannel would reach. "You don't have to go over there unless they call you." She rested her forehead against his spine and breathed their combined musk.

"What kind of reporter are you? Aren't you curious?"

"My paper doesn't come out till Thursday. I've got forty-eight hours to get the story."

Something crashed, and smoke puffed up and dissipated. Calen wrestled the window shut. Walking out of her embrace, he fumbled in the dimness for his clothes, most of them festooning the Boston rocker beside the closet.

After a moment's irresolution, Maxey went to the bureau and collected underwear, sweatpants, and sweatshirt by the feeble illumination from the lamp across the street. If she went with him, she wouldn't be lying in bed wondering how much longer he'd be gone.

They switched on a light in the kitchen to come home to and tramped down the steep inside stairs to the front door. As they crossed the porch, Maxey saw her downstairs neighbor Oliver Kraig peeping out between the lace edges of his door curtains. She saluted him, and he nodded, his old man face floating ghostly behind the glass.

Their feet crunched a carpet of leaves, off the curb, across the street, up the curb, and through the side yard of neighbors Maxey had never met. A high board fence blocked out the alley, but it contained a gate with a simple hook and eye latch. Calen opened it and led Maxey into a knot of firefighters in full turnouts except for gas masks. At either end of the alley, emergency vehicles blinked lights and crackled radio communications. Flaccid hoses cluttered the asphalt.

"Howdy, Calen," one of the firemen called.

"Looks like you've got it knocked down already," he answered.

The alley here bulged wider than most alleys, allowing for modest parking lots behind the businesses. The fire scene was one building west of where they stood. The rear wall, cement block, contained one small door, one garage-type door, and one window missing most of its glass. The smaller door hung in pieces, probably split lengthwise by a fireman's ax. A blackness darker than shadows surrounded it. While Maxey watched, two firemen emerged and motioned for another to come inside.

The man who had hailed Calen stepped closer to converse. "We were lucky on this one. A cop was patrolling the alley when the thing flared up, so we got on it right away. Confined it to the back, here. Could have been a heck of a lot worse. Place is full of mattresses."

Calen nodded and turned to look at the building again. "Oh, hell," he muttered.

Maxey twisted to see what he'd seen and realized it was, instead, what he'd smelled. A sickening sweet stench wafted past them up the alley. At that moment, the three firemen who'd gone inside rushed out the door. The youngest-looking, rosy-cheeked one shouted, "Marshall Taylor, we've got a body in here."

Calen strode to meet them, and they huddled in the middle of the alley. Then one of the firemen peeled off toward the patrol car barricading the end of the alley, and Calen and the other two trooped through the charred entry. The rest of the firefighters began to hoist hoses and carry their gear to the truck. Wanting to cover her nose in case the smell came swirling back, Maxey rocked from foot to foot, arms hugging her middle.

She became aware of voices behind her and realized a number of Spruce Street residents had gathered on back porches and lawns. A freckle-faced woman with one thick gray braid down her back leaned in the gateway Maxey and Calen had used.

"Is that the futon place?" Maxey asked her.

"Either that or the office supply. They're in the same building. Did I hear them say somebody died in there?"

Maxey nodded.

The woman lapped her silver and black Rockies' jacket tighter. "Well, all my family's accounted for," she said as she backed away and let the gate squeak shut.

The fireman and the policeman he'd gone to fetch walked up the alley just as Calen swung out of the entryway. There were more consultations, the policeman talked into his radio, the fireman began to unwind yellow plastic tape to cordon off the scene, and Calen hurried toward Maxey.

"I've got to get my evidence kit."

She quick-stepped behind him through the fence, the yard, and along the street to his white station wagon. "One victim?"

"Hope that's all." He found the hatch key in his pants pocket and lifted the door, leaning inside to drag out a black canvas bag. "You go on back to bed. This'll take a while."

She wanted to kiss him, but she settled for patting his cheek before he turned away. All business, he wouldn't have reciprocated the kiss anyway.

Back upstairs, she replaced the sweats with her robe, piled both pillows against the headboard, and settled down to read a 1989 *Atlantic* she'd gotten off the public library free table. Every few paragraphs, her mind skidded somewhere else, mostly to Calen, who'd be down on one knee in the smelly, damp ashes, looking for clues to the killer fire.

A door clicked shut and Maxey came full awake. Weak morning light spread through the unshaded window, illuminating Calen, dancing on one foot as he tried to extricate his other leg from his pants.

"Phew. You smell like brimstone," Maxey welcomed him.

"I get tired of the same old bay rum." He wadded the pants under one arm pit and went to work on the buttons of his shirt.

"Who died in the fire?"

"Let me take a shower first. I'll tell you the details over breakfast."

She rolled her eyes. "Good. I'm trying to cut back on how much I eat."

Maxey walked into the *Blatant Regard* office and smiled to see Scotty already at the keyboard, typing like a man about to shout, "Stop the presses!" The keys didn't hesitate in their rattle as he shouted, instead, "Morning, Ms. Burnell."

"Morning, Mr. Springer. Hot story?" She knew it wasn't. He always typed like that.

Just as he always arrived for work early and left late and did his share of the grunt work—a refreshing change from her last business partner, Reece Macey. Another difference between the men was that Scotty wasn't Maxey's philandering ex-husband who'd left for Alaska to seek his fortune.

Maxey headed toward the coffee pot that Scotty had remembered to put on the perk. The rich, humid scent filled the room with Brazilian incense.

Scotty one-fingered the enter key with a flourish, and swiveled around to grin at her. His red plaid shirt clashed with his salt and chili-pepper hair. His blue eyes sparkled from a frame of crow's feet. He needed a shave. He was short, too thin, more than twice her age, and if it hadn't been for Calen, Maxey might have asked him to marry her.

"I'm writing a man-on-the-street survey I did yesterday," Scotty said. "What mall-crawlers will be wearing for Halloween."

Maxey leaned against the table and blew into her coffee. "Every day is Halloween on Pearl Street, what with the New Agers and the flower children and the punkers. They'll have to dress like conservative Republicans to be costumed."

"And a scary costume that would be, too. How about you?"

"I don't know. An old sheet with eye-holes is about my creative speed."

"No, I mean what are you working on today. What's your story du jour?"

She carried her cup to her desk and switched on the monitor.

"There was a fire at the Futon Lode early this morning. I can compose a few eyewitness comments about that. You could see it from my window."

"Much damage?"

"Not to the building, but it did a lot of damage to the guy that was in it. He's dead."

"Oh-oh. The owner?"

Maxey yawned, shaking her head. "Owner's friend. Or acquaintance, at least. This guy, Basil Underwood, came into the store late Monday. He needed a place to crash for the night, so Derrick Sikes—he's the store owner—let him bed down on some of the merchandise in the back room. Calen thinks Underwood was smoking, in spite of promising Sikes he wouldn't, and he probably fell asleep."

"Cigarettes." Scotty shook his head in disgust. "One of the leading causes of statistics."

"Is that a quotation?"

He shut one eye and thought. "'Nothing is said that has not been said before.' Terence, around one-fifty B.C."

"Right. Words and oxygen—the first recyclables."

"Is that a quotation?"

"If you use it, it will be. Spell my name right."

"Very nice," Scotty said, pretending to jot it down on his scratch pad. "So what happened with the deceased lady you released from the hospital yesterday?"

"Sylvia Wellman. Poor woman. I ought to write an obituary for her. Give her a posthumous, Warhol fifteen minutes."

"Considering that you were her closest friend, don't you think it'll be rough, tracking down any information on her?"

"No Pulitzer Prize comes easy." Maxey swallowed the last of her coffee. "Wasn't there a song titled *Who Was Sylvia*?"

"*Who Is Sylvia*. Franz Schubert." Scotty's answer trailed off as he returned his attention to Halloween, Boulder, Colorado-style. After a few minutes he began to hum something ponderous. *Who Is Sylvia*, no doubt.

Maxey stared at the black screen that awaited her command. A couple of years ago, she was in much the same position as poor Sylvia—not dead, but except for her useless ex-husband, alone. In rapid succession she'd found Calen and Scotty. What the hell, she'd even found the father she thought had died long ago, though for all practical purposes, Deon Burnell was still as good as dead to her, avoiding her like the proverbial plague, up in Wyoming.

According to the release Maxey had signed yesterday, Sylvia's next stop was Kelliher Brothers Funeral Home. Maxey reached for the phone book. With Scotty's key-banging providing background cacophony, Maxey spoke to one of the Kellihers.

"I'd like to know when you're—ah—burying Sylvia Wellman."

Mr. Kelliher's voice did an excellent James Jones impersonation, every syllable present and accounted for. "The funeral's this afternoon at three. No viewing, no memorial service, interment only, at Mountain View Cemetery."

Maxey thanked him and disconnected. Then she stared at the blank computer screen again, fingers expectant on home position. Which story first? Sylvia Wellman or Basil Underwood?

Finally, she abandoned the empty file and called up the city council meeting report she'd been editing. Writing about deadly dull held more appeal than writing about just plain dead.

Bright blue sky, orange and yellow trees, red carnations in a green metal can—the scene seemed too colorful for a funeral. Maxey had brought the flowers, and it was a good thing, too, or Sylvia would have had none. Maxey had expected a plot back in a far corner, wedged in among other graves of unloved ones. Instead, Sylvia would lie in almost the center of the cemetery, a neighbor's bas relief angel facing her way.

Funeral director Kelliher might have been called Mount Kelliher. Tall, broad-chested, and craggy-faced, he made Maxey welcome by enclosing her hand in both of his and squeezing gently.

Although he looked as if he could carry one end of the casket by himself, he did have a kid with a Bart Simpson haircut and two cemetery employees in bib overalls to help him move it from the hearse to the grave site. There was no tent, no chairs, no minister. No mourners except Maxey. Still, Sylvia arrived in a copper-colored casket instead of plain wood or plastic. Happy for her, but a bit puzzled, Maxey stood with her back to the southern sun, brown rayon skirt flapping around her knees. Mr. Kelliher asked if she wanted to say a few words, and she shook her head.

The two cemetery employees lurked a few yards distant, ready to move in and fill the grave when the little party dispersed. Which, since Maxey had nothing to say, it did without further ceremony. The kid had already left the scene, how or in what direction Maxey hadn't noticed.

She walked beside Mr. Kelliher through the dry grass toward her white Toyota, which looked like a scruffy tugboat anchored in front of the sleek battleship hearse.

"Do you know anything about Ms. Wellman? Who she was?" Maxey asked.

Kelliher cleared his throat, and the rich, deep voice surged out of it. "No, I can't say that I do. You aren't related to her?"

She shook her head. "I never met her."

The grass crackled under their shoes. She could feel him wondering about her, but it was too much trouble to explain.

"I believe I recognize you as the lady who owns that little alternative newspaper on Pearl Street."

"The *Blatant Regard*, yes."

"Surely you've met the deceased, then. She spent all her time walking downtown. Black-haired woman, rather stocky, never smiling, never saying anything, a flowered dress under a tan, fringed suede jacket, no matter what the weather?"

"That's Sylvia Wellman? The only name I ever knew her by was Packy." Maxey thought a moment. "That explains how she had my business card. She was always roaming from business to business, picking up any freebies on the counters. Sometimes she'd exchange stuff. Like she'd take a toothpick at one place, then leave it and take a brochure at another place, so the merchants started calling her Packy. What a sad way to waste one's life."

They reached the driveway and Maxey paused with Kelliher beside the hearse. "Who reimburses you for indigent burials? The county?"

He nodded. "Social Services. But Miss Wellman wasn't indigent. She had some funds to pay for my services and the cemetery space."

"Huh. To look at her, you'd have sworn she didn't have the price of her next meal."

Kelliher smiled a gloomy smile. "Perhaps she's one

of those eccentric millionaires with a mattress full of cash."

Maxey's imagination was off and running. "Who would inherit if she did? She didn't have a will, you can bet. If she really had no relatives, would the state get it all?"

Kelliher chuckled. "If she really had it in her mattress, the mice and roaches will have taken care of it by now. She roomed at the Bluebell House."

"Right. I saw that on the release I signed. I guess that's why I thought she was indigent. Why someone with any money would live in a place like that—"

"We are fortunate in Boulder to have very few disadvantaged areas. That one apartment house must comprise about eighty per cent of our slums."

"And a big wedge of the city's crime, too. If Sylvia had a money mattress, it's probably in the paws of two-legged vermin by now."

Maxey took Iris Avenue to Broadway and drove south to Boulder Community Hospital. She remembered the name of the woman who had phoned her about releasing Packy's—Sylvia's—body, because her name was so apt. Patience, in Administration.

The hospital hummed with mechanical and human activity. It smelled like floor wax and rubbing alcohol. Maxey picked her way through a warren of halls to Patience, who turned out to be a narrow-faced young woman in a burgundy dress that hung too long and too loose on her angular figure. When Maxey found her, Patience was entering her office with an armload of file folders hugged to her small chest. Adding the stack to her already buried desk, Patience caught the top folder before it could slide off the summit, and waited for Maxey to state her business.

"I wondered if you might have more information about the lady whose body you asked me to release to the funeral home yesterday morning. Sylvia Wellman. Did she really have no one else to do that for her?"

Patience rubbed her nose and grinned at the floor. "To

tell you the truth, I picked you at random. There were a whole handful of business cards to choose from. In her pencil box."

"Pencil box?"

Patience adjusted a shoulder pad and motioned Maxey to sit down before slumping into her own chair behind the messy desk. "Pencil box. Cigar box. Whatever you'd call it. She didn't bring a purse with her."

"I guess I never saw her carry a purse. She usually had a white plastic grocery bag though. The kind with handles."

"Oh, so you did know her. That's good."

"I didn't know her well enough. I wish now I'd been nicer to her. A smile never hurt nobody." Maxey gave one to Patience, to prove it.

Patience smiled back. "Everything I know about Sylvia was on the release form—her address and phone number, when she was admitted, when she died, the cause of death, who her doctor was. Maybe he could tell you more. Dr. Rudderly, I think it was."

"And the pencil box. Her personal effects. What happened to them?"

"They're in unclaimed property. You want them?"

"Are you allowed to give them to me?"

"I don't see why not. You signed her out. It's not like there's a gold nugget or a lottery ticket in there. The little box itself is about the best of the lot, and it might be worth seventy-five cents."

"Yes, let me have it."

"Good. Be right back."

Maxey day dreamed across the little, windowless room at a computer monitor weaving screen-saver geometrics. She wondered if it could put a susceptible person into a trance. Fortunately, Patience came sweeping back before Maxey determined her own hypnotic threshold.

"Here. See?" Patience held out the all-red, all-plastic box and snapped open the lid.

Maxey poked a forefinger inside to stir the contents. Business cards, rubber bands, paper clips, scraps of adding machine tape, a feather—

"Hey, a nickel," Patience crowed. "Maybe I shouldn't give the box to you after all."

Maxey shut it and tucked it under her arm as she stood. "Thanks. Watch for my article in the *Regard*."

"Wait. You have to sign."

Patience pointed out the correct line on another kind of release form, and Maxey thanked her again before embarking on a journey around the innards of the building in search of an exit.

Out in the parking lot, she unlocked the Toyota, considering her next move. She ought to go back to the office and write the rest of her stories for tomorrow's deadline. Still, she needed more information for the one about Sylvia, and the disreputable Bluebell House couldn't be more than a dozen blocks away.

2

The ringing telephone caught Scotty in the middle of a stretch. He let his chair thump forward and reached to answer it.

"It's me," Maxey's voice announced. "I don't think I'm going to make it back to the office before five, so when I'm through running around, I'll just go home instead. Okay?"

"It's up to you and your conscience. You're on salary, right? Writing a story about going fishing, are we?"

She didn't rise to his teasing. "Don't forget to unplug the coffee pot."

"Honey, I've been unplugging coffee pots since before you were born."

"I found out who Sylvia was. You know the woman who wandered around downtown picking up free stuff at businesses? Packy?"

"Right. That was Sylvia?"

"Right. One more favor, Scotty?"

He sighed extra loud into the mouthpiece.

Maxey ignored this, too. "If you're stopping at the Dilly Deli on your way home, would you ask Morrie if he has any Packy stories? He's a nice guy. He'll say something touchingly quotable for my article."

"Okay. See you tomorrow."

"Wait a minute, Scotty. Maybe I ought to mention where I'm going. Just in case."

"In case of what?"

"I'm going to interview some people at the Bluebell House."

"Oh, Jeez, Maxey. Don't you have anything better to do? Maybe I ought to meet you there."

"No, I'll be fine. No kidding."

"How about calling me at home tonight? So I can stop worrying that the partnership has suddenly become a sole proprietorship?"

"Okay, I'll phone you around eight. You can tell me what Morrie said, and I'll start the write-up tonight."

"Like I said, don't you have anything better to do?"

"It's that or clean the oven."

"Wait a minute. Let me get this straight. Ovens have to be cleaned?"

"God, Scotty. You sound more like my ex-husband every day."

Twenty-five minutes later, Scotty shrugged into his faded denim jacket, disconnected the coffee pot, shut off most of the lights, and stepped out on the pedestrian walkway. As he locked the front door and turned east, the perfume of garlic and tomatoes invited him to cross over to Old Chicago for supper. A little farther on, the more exotic spices of Mid-Eastern dishes invaded his nose.

He kept walking. The Deli would have some mighty fine aromas, too. It was his favorite take-out after a day of slaving over a hot computer.

If someone had told him a year ago that he'd be working a regular job with a good-looking young woman, instead of playing handyman in more ways than one with a fair-looking old woman, he'd have laughed and ordered another beer. The day he met Maxey, in the bathroom, of all places, he'd been living with her Aunt Janet on what was left of her family farm in Nebraska. It wasn't Maxey's fault that things went sour between Janet and him. He'd been thinking the time had come to move on, and the job opening in Boulder, Colorado cinched it. He'd never entertained any romantic notions about Maxey, in spite of her blonde hair and nice figure and cheery attitude. Nope—too old for her, damn it. Besides, she'd found herself a real nice fella in Calen the Arson Detective.

Scotty wondered if Janet was using the clothesline he'd put up for her, and whether she would spoil the moment by bitching and groaning if he called her up just to say hi. Who was that Frenchman that said the heaviest object in the world is the body of the woman you've ceased to love? For sure it was Lord Chesterfield who said the only lasting peace between a man and a woman is doubtless a separation.

He strolled behind a grunge of teens engaged in a flurry of shoving, laughing, and gratuitous cursing. Baggy pants, baggy shirts, and high top sneakers with the laces dragging. Their entrance would make any store manager cringe. Scotty was relieved that they didn't turn in at the Deli.

The bell above the door heralded his entrance, and Morrie, fat brown fingers splayed around five cans of pop destined for a table in the far corner, jerked his chin in recognition. The white and chrome room sparkled like an operating theater, but it smelled like Scotty's mother's kitchen miles and years distant—like warm bread and sausage, with just a hint of Windex underneath.

At the carry-out counter, Scotty stuffed his hands into the back pockets of his jeans, planted his feet, and rocked onto his heels, waiting for his turn behind a six-foot duck. It was probably a Halloween costume, but on the Pearl Street Mall, one never knew. Sondra, Morrie's hired help, took the bird's order with efficient disinterest.

Morrie returned from delivering the soft drinks and paused beside Scotty. The same general size and shape as the duck, Morrie had a smile as real as a three-year-old's, and it was almost always in place. His brown, balding head reflected the overhead fluorescent bulbs as he bent to pick up a straw wrapper from the gleaming floor.

"Which of your usuals would you like tonight?" he asked.

"Chili and a Caesar salad."

"Hold the croutons?"

"That or I can pick 'em off myself."

The duck, two large white sacks under each wing, waddled out. Scotty moved up to the counter and leaned on it, watching Morrie dip out his order. "You know the woman that folks called 'Packy?' Stout lady with short, black hair and—" He stopped, because Morrie was nodding. "Well, she died a couple days ago and Maxey is writing a little memorial piece about her. Got any personal recollections that would be good for a eulogy?"

Morrie snapped the plastic lid on the chili, thinking. "I could say some stuff not for publication."

"She gave you trouble?"

"Not me. Some of the restaurants along here wouldn't let her in. Said she was bad for business. The way she looked and acted, you know—scruffy and sour-faced. Never buying anything. Walking the streets all the time."

"Was she a prostitute?"

"Aww, no, I don't think a prossy. Just a street person. Homeless, except she had a place to live. She'd come in here and take a napkin or a packet of sweetener and leave. Once in a while she did buy a sandwich or a coffee."

"What was her voice like?"

"Just what you'd expect, looking at her. Real low and kind of gruff."

"Any accent?"

Morrie shook his head, set the carry-out on the counter and rang it up. "She didn't say enough for a person to tell."

Sondra came up beside her boss and leaned toward Scotty. "I heard about these guys that were messing with Packy—jerks from school. Following her down the street and calling her names and throwing trash at her and generally being bad-ass flake-heads. She finally turned around and goes, 'I got a bomb here.' In her plastic grocery bag, you know? Course they didn't believe that, so they hooted and carried on till she reached in the bag and pulled it out."

"A bomb?" Scotty exclaimed.

"Hand grenade." Sondra grinned. "Probably a toy. They weren't that loony to find out. Backed off and let her march on down the street. Wish I could've seen their faces."

Morrie shook his head, his mouth dragged down at the corners. "That woman had some kind of grail complex—spent all her time looking and not finding."

Scotty pocketed his change and lifted his bag of soup n' salad. "Maxey said you'd know what to say."

Bluebell House had been built as a private mansion, the pride of a gold mining family when Boulder was young. Three stories high and half a block long, all heavy tan stone, deep porches, and zigzag roof lines, it must have been ostentatious, even by gold mine owners' standards. Now it clung to its hill at the intersection of two narrow streets, surrounded by mean-looking run-down houses with cramped, neglected yards, like an avalanche about to happen.

Maxey found a weedy asphalt parking lot behind the Bluebell. There were plenty of spaces, probably because the residents were forced to put food and shelter before that other basic need, wheels. The sun was a thing of the past here in the lap of the foothills. The individual shadows had all oozed together into one big twilight. Dim lights struggled out of assorted windows, many of which stood open, their sills cluttered with bottles and cans and dangling towels and underwear.

At the far northwest end of the lot, a sextet of gangling, muscled bodies fought to dribble and shoot a basketball at a hoop that was nothing but rim, on a post so wobbly, it presented a moving target.

Locking the Toyota, Maxey struck out toward the brown double doors in the center of the building, pretending she knew where she was going and expected to get there unmolested. The door squealed as she dragged it open. Three of the four bulbs in the lamp above the stairway inside were burned out.

The smell wasn't as bad as she'd expected. Old cooking grease, mostly. She marched up gritty stairs to the beat of rap music thumping from someone's speakers. At the top she paused to get her bearings. There wasn't anything so obviously helpful as a sign with an arrow reading *Manager*. The dim hall stretched left and right, lined with doors, many of them open, like a dormitory. The battered linoleum floor creaked as she crossed it to knock on the open frame of number twenty-three.

"Hello?" she called, trying not to look too closely at the stains on the carpet just across the threshold.

Not disappointed that no one answered, she moved on down the hall to another door ajar. Before she could knock, a man came running down a staircase at the far end of the hall. Fingers snapping, shoulders rolling, he jiggle-pranced toward Maxey, who was relieved to see he wasn't under the influence of anything more sinister than the cassette player plugged into his ears.

Waving to get his attention, she raised her voice. "Could you tell me where Sylvia Wellman used to live?"

Without a pause in his routine, he jabbed a forefinger twice at the ceiling and danced on out of Maxey's life.

She climbed up the flight of wooden stairs to a clone of the hall below, including the Gothic-grim lighting and scarred linoleum. A trio of swarthy young men wearing denim, cowboy boots, and hostile stares lounged against the wall to her right. One of them spat on the floor before she turned the other direction.

Feeling eyes crawling on her back, Maxey stopped at the first open doorway and raised a fist to knock before she saw the old man sitting on the bed. "Excuse me? I'm looking for someone who knew Sylvia Wellman."

He folded his arms and lifted his head with the deliberation of someone submerged in water. His gaze didn't quite focus on where she stood.

"Sylvia Wellman?" she prompted.

He freed one hand and languidly waved it. As she walked the direction he'd seemed to indicate, the guys down the hall laughed like pirates—har, har, har.

Across the hall, a younger man opened a door and peered out. "Need some help?" he asked, his smile wide, his eyes hopeful. His red pullover sweater had something yellow dribbled down the front.

"I'm trying to find where Sylvia Wellman lived." Her smile felt false. She wished she was at home cleaning her oven.

"Oh, you're on the wrong floor. She was three hundred. Come on, I'll show you."

Slipping into the hall, he shut the door, not before Maxey glimpsed a sway-backed couch smothered in magazines, newspapers, books, and balls of wadded paper. He had a stooped, rushing gait, one giant-step for every two Maxey-steps. His thinning black hair stood up all around as if he'd just ripped off a stocking cap. His unusually white skin might indicate recent illness or a bout of prison—or just naturally pale skin. He kept turning to look at Maxey, whose nervousness led her to ask such dumb questions as, "Are there any children living here?"

"No, no, no children allowed. No pets either." He swayed closer, hand by his mouth shielding the confidence as he added, "No overnight guests, either, if you get my drift. All rules observed in their flagrant non-observation. You follow me?" He laughed. "Well of course you're following me. Right up these steps."

They'd come to yet another stairwell, narrower than the others but just as grimy underfoot. Her guide took the risers three at a time and then waited at the summit for her to catch up. Someone's television swelled a soap opera theme.

"This is the attic," he said, watching her look around. "Not as many rooms. Not as nice." He demonstrated by stretching up and touching the ceiling. From the black fingerprints already there, this was apparently a ritual part of the tour.

"Uh-huh. And Sylvia—"

"Right here. First door."

She'd expected it to be locked, but the man reached past her and opened it, giving an extra shove that sent it bouncing off the wall behind. Then he snapped on the light, one buggy globe in the center of the water-marked ceiling.

"No one else has moved in yet?" Maxey asked the obvious as she leaned to examine the little room. It was crowded with furniture but empty of life.

"Naw. Go on in. It's okay."

It might have been okay, but it didn't seem completely prudent. Maxey wanted to thank her companion and send him home, but he pushed inside on her heels and stood by, as helpful as if she were considering renting it herself.

A fourth of the space was taken up by the single bed. Maple, with a stained, blue and white ticking-striped mattress, it hunkered below two, double-hung windows, only one of which rated a tipsy Venetian blind. Another fourth of the space involved a black vinyl recliner chair with cracked arms and a floor lamp without a shade. And one fourth loomed as a wardrobe. There was no need to walk over and open it. All the doors and drawers hung open on emptiness.

"You a relative?" the man asked.

"No. I'm from a local newspaper. I'm writing her obituary."

"No kidding? What newspaper? Don't tell me. I recognize you now from the photo on your column. The *Regard*. Am I right?" He bounced from foot to foot, as thrilled as if she'd said she was from CNN.

Nodding, Maxey studied the last fourth of Sylvia's room. It might have been called a kitchenette—a chipped white sink and a gray metal table with a top carved full of initials and obscene graffiti.

"What's your name?" the man demanded.

"Maxey." She tried smiling again. "What's yours?"

"Robert Truet, but you can call me Roberto Trueblood.

That's my pseudonym."

Oh-oh. Here's where he would announce he was a writer. Science fiction, she bet.

"I write poetry." He waited for her to applaud.

"Good for you." She hesitated a polite beat before changing the subject. "She didn't have a stove or refrigerator?"

"Residents may have hot plates. In the winter, we hang stuff out the windows to keep cold."

"Ahh. And the bathroom?"

"Up the hall. Toilets and shower stalls. I'll show you."

"No, that's okay," she assured him and flailed about for another change of subject. "Did Sylvia have a best friend in the building? Someone I could interview?"

"Georgiana Flint." Robert nodded and nodded, as if expecting to be contradicted.

"Does she live here?"

"Next door up the hall."

"Well, thank you for your help." Maxey headed for the door. "I'll have a few words with Ms. Flint, and then I'll—"

Robert scurried out ahead of her and hurried up the hall to knock at the next room. Maxey forced down her irritation as she followed him. He probably didn't get many visitors. Naturally he'd want to wring this opportunity dry.

When his knocking failed to raise a response, he grinned back over his shoulder at Maxey. "She's in there. Maybe out of it, but in there." He sniffed with great exaggeration. "Smell it? She's in love with her booze. Could be swacked, in which case, you won't get nada."

Maxey reached past him to rap smartly on the dull wooden door. She couldn't picture herself coming back up here tomorrow, and not just because of the *Regard*'s implacable deadline.

"What!" a deep voice complained from the other side.

"Coming in, Georgie," Robert shouted as he turned the knob and opened the door on darkness that stank of sour liquor and chronic illness.

"Get the hell out of my room." The voice came from near the center.

Undaunted, Robert walked inside and fumbled a hand down the wall, searching for the light switch.

Maxey waited in the hall, vowing to herself to at least *buy* some damned oven cleaner.

The overhead globe burst on, disclosing a room as small and uninviting as Sylvia's, the main difference being the woman curled up in the split vinyl recliner.

Maxey had expected her to be elderly. Georgiana looked forty, and she was probably younger than that. Her frowzy brown hair stuck out from her head wider than her shoulders did from her skinny body. Her face gleamed as white as aspen bark in the harsh light. Her shadowed, sunken eyes, like knot holes, watched without expression as Robert waved Maxey in.

Maxey paused on the threshold, unwilling to intrude on this woman's obvious sorrows. "Please excuse me, Ms. Flint. I was told you were a friend of Sylvia Wellman."

"What of it?" She reached into the chair by her hip and drew an amber bottle into the lap of her pink chenille bathrobe.

"I'm writing an obituary for the newspaper. Is there anything you could—"

"There isn't any money. No jewelry. She didn't give me nothing. So don't you say she did."

"No, I wasn't interested in—"

"She didn't ever have anything valuable. Never! Any yahoo that thought otherwise was sadly mistaken. That's how she lived and that's how she died—for nothing." Georgiana slid the bottle into the neckline of the robe, between her breasts.

Maxey shook her head. "I'm not interested in—"

"Not her daughter are you?"

"No. Did she have a daughter?"

"Who the hell cares."

"Did Sylvia have a family somewhere?"

Georgiana shrugged, and the bottle softly sloshed. "Why don't you ask me if I have a family."

Robert, who'd been following the conversation with rapt attention, looking from woman to woman, snorted. "Everybody knows the story of how you're the last of the Flints. How the entire family got wiped out in a car wreck except you because you'd been grounded for getting all D's on your report card."

Maxey sucked in a breath, shocked at Robert's callousness.

Georgiana gazed into the distance and belched gently.

"Didn't Sylvia give you any of her treasures?" Robert twisted to wink at Maxey.

"No."

"Come on, George. Tell the truth."

"Don't call me George," she said. She squeezed herself into a tighter ball and called Robert names worse than George. He covered both ears and sang-shouted *Jingle Bells* until Georgiana's lips stopped moving.

Maxey decided that if Robert called her Max, she would plant her fist in his stomach and run. "I'm sorry we bothered you, Ms. Flint," she said, backing toward the door.

"She was the only one who treated me nice," Georgiana said, her voice trembling on the edge of a wail. "And then she went and died and left me like the rest. Just like the goddamned rest."

"Your cursing is so appealing," Robert said. "A filthy mouth is so *tres* attractive.

"Thank you for your time," Maxey said, motioning testily at Robert to exit. She motioned more vigorously as she saw Georgiana lunge toward the side of the chair.

Georgiana didn't vomit, though. She patted the floor under the recliner. "Wait," she snarled. "Take this garbage with you." She hauled out a yellow plastic cigar box and held it out, shaking it with impatience when Maxey didn't move. "I don't want it. Throw it in a dumpster on your way out."

Maxey crossed the thready rug to take the box and lift the lid. Except for the color, it was a twin to the one Patience had given her. It held an equally scruffy assortment of the objects people throw into junk drawers.

"Even if it is her best one, I don't want it," Georgiana grumbled.

"Best one?"

Georgiana shifted her hips in an angry flounce. "She had this system. Filing system, she called it. Pick up the stuff in the plastic bag, come home and put it in the red box, once a month file the best items in this yellow box. I was her banker, see. Her safety deposit vault." She sniffed. "Crazy old bag. Crazier than I am, and that's saying a lot."

Startled, Maxey looked across the open box, down into Georgiana's glittering eyes. For one unblinking moment, she saw intelligence and humor there.

"Don't you want to keep this to remember her—"

"I don't want to remember her. Take it and get out."

"Well, thanks again." Maxey retreated, the box in both hands in front of her.

"Just don't give it to anybody else. Sylvia would kill me." Georgiana fumbled with her robe, trying to withdraw the bottle, unconcerned that she exposed one flaccid breast in the process.

Maxey herded Robert ahead of her into the hall.

"Shut the light out, damn it," Georgiana shouted after them.

When Robert just grinned and kept walking, Maxey turned back to fulfill the request. As she pulled shut the door, Georgiana's wet, hacking cough hurt Maxey's chest just to hear it. She rushed toward the stairwell, Sylvia's box tucked under one arm.

"Careful. This is the murder weapon," Robert said, waving her forward, still smiling like an idiot.

Maxey, about to take the first step down the wooden stairs, froze and looked around. "What are you talking about?"

"Under your foot there. Sylvia fell down this flight."

"Oh. But it wasn't murder."

"Oh. Of course not." He cocked his head and wiggled his eyebrows.

The sounds of reggae music and male laughter burst out and were immediately muffled as someone on the second floor opened and shut a door. Maxey started down, trailing a hand along the railing, ready to grab it if Robert made any sudden, irrational moves.

In the lower hallway, a man and woman groped one another outside the party room. As Maxey strode past, the man buried his face in the woman's neck and dipped her backwards. His hand, quick as a lizard, pinched Maxey's rear.

Giggling, Robert followed her to the next stairwell.

"Good-bye, Robert," she said, succumbing to full retreat now. Her shoes hammered against the stairs, and Robert's scuffled right behind her.

"Wait," he gasped as they hit the first floor hall. He grabbed her sleeve, and she jerked it away before whirling around to frown at him. "Listen, Maxey, I wanted to show you some of my poems."

She'd known this was coming for the last half hour. Mentally gritting her teeth, she kept walking. "Sorry. I don't have time for that."

"That's no problem. I'll bring them to the office."

"No!" She forced her voice to a more polite decibel. "I mean, the *Regard* doesn't print poetry. Sorry."

"Well, maybe the *Regard* has never published poetry up to now, but once you've read my stuff, you'll change the policy. I don't even expect any money for them. A tear sheet would be nice though."

"No, Robert. No."

She'd reached the brink of the short stairway that led to the double doors to the parking lot. As her left foot reached out into space, Robert gripped her upper arm and pushed.

Still holding on, he yanked her back again. Heart skittering, she clung to the banister with one hand and hit at him with the other.

"Whoa, you gotta be careful there," Robert said. "You okay?"

She had dropped Sylvia's box. It lay on its side halfway down the flight, dribbling paper clips and rubber bands and scraps of paper down the steps. One ebony marble hopped toward the front door and lost itself in the dirty shadows.

More angry than frightened, Maxey descended as far as the box, scooped it up, swept in a handful of Sylvia's valuables, and ran the rest of the way down. She left the marble to its fate.

3

Maxey found Calen sprawled on her living room couch, a paperback in one hand, the other hand massaging Moe's jowls as the cat lolled, groggy with pleasure, across his lap.

It was the fourth night in a row that Calen had come by and made himself at home, a new record that Maxey didn't want to jinx by commenting upon. He owned a little bi-level house in the Table Mesa part of town. They'd never discussed moving in together there or here. Since Maxey had no desire for children, she took a hedonist attitude: If a relationship ain't broke, don't fix it.

"Had supper yet?" she asked.

Moe lifted one eyelid and slowly rolled it shut again.

Calen shook his head and raised his arm, book and all, to look at his watch. "Want to send out for a pizza?"

"Sure."

She made the call, and then she telephoned Scotty to report in. After jotting down the "grail complex" quote from Morrie, she carried her notebook to the couch and settled next to Calen. He tented the book on his knee, dropped his arm around her shoulders and nuzzled her ear lobe. She felt her muscles go as slack as Moe's.

They leaned heads together for a long time, listening for the pizza man, listening to Moe's snoring. Maxey hoped that heaven was like this—a quiet time of doing nothing with the one you love.

She found it hard to believe she'd ever been happy before Calen materialized in her life. On her own one morning, she'd been looking for a news story in a burned-down house, and there he was, on his own, investigating the basement for arson. Instead of chasing her off, he'd showed her the clue he'd found. It wasn't love at first sight, or even fifth. But now for Maxey, it was love at *every* sight of his crisp graying hair, his intelligent eyes, his warm mouth—and all points below. He seemed to think she was pretty nifty, too. But given her luck with previous relationships, she couldn't shake off the worry that Calen was too good to be true.

"A wooden nickle for your thoughts," he said.

Maxey sighed before she lied, "I have to write up the story about the Futon Lode fire. You got anything new on it?"

"There was no indication of any accelerant. We think Underwood was smoking in bed, so to speak." Calen sat up straighter. "There's no sprinkler system in that old building. The smoke detector batteries had never been changed. What we have is one more case of negligence and carelessness and downright dumbness."

"Not arson, huh. No fires in any other part of the building?"

"Nope."

"Front and back doors locked when the firefighters arrived?"

"Yep."

"Who owns the building?"

"A corporation in Denver. Nothing suspicious there." He wrapped his hand around the back of her neck, which always made her feel delightfully small and cherished. "So okay if we call it accidental?"

"I guess."

She shut her eyes and wrote the headline and first sentence in her head: *Man Dies in Futon Fire. Take the warn-*

ing seriously—cigarettes can be hazardous to your health.

Maxey walked to work on Wednesday because she wanted to stop at various shops along the way to get quotes for her Basil Underwood and Sylvia Wellman stories.

The logical first stop was the Futon Lode.

Fire Sale, announced a computer print-out banner taped to the show window. The front door was locked, and Maxey glanced at her watch. It didn't do her any good to know the time, because no business hours were posted. She backed away and looked at the plate glass display window of the neighboring office supply.

A black velvet curtain backdropped a display of briefcases, desks, chairs, and skeletons. The skeletons—the cardboard kind with brass brad movable joints—hung by fishing line from a chicken wire ceiling, all dozen of them in the same unimaginative pose dictated by gravity. The limp line-up didn't influence Maxey toward the purchase of any new office equipment.

On the entrance, a large plastic red and white sign seemed to shout its welcome: *OPEN COME IN.*

It smelled of coffee inside, with a faint underlayer of old smoke. Rows and rows of office supplies waited to organize someone's life—red boxes of file folders, green boxes of adhesive tape, yellow packages of legal pads, and a rainbow of pens and pencils. At the back, a wide staircase led up to an open expanse of mezzanine, the furniture department, apparently. Maxey glimpsed desks and chairs in sedate tans and grays through the balcony railing.

"Hello. Could I help you?" The woman had been kneeling in a cross aisle, threading boxes of typewriter ribbons onto a pegboard hook.

"Good morning. I'm Maxey Burnell from the *Blatant Regard*. I was going to interview your neighbor about the fire. Do you know what time he opens?"

The woman stood up, unbending slowly, joint by joint. As she approached Maxey, the lines in her face and the gray in her short, frizzy hair came into focus.

"That boy opens whenever he feels like it, is the best I can promise you." She sniffed. "Not the way to run a business. Don't quote me."

Maxey smiled. "Okay. Could I quote you on something else, though? Are you the owner of—" Maxey was embarrassed to realize she didn't know the name of the store.

"Yes. My husband and I. For thirty-nine years." She drew up taller.

"That's wonderful," Maxey said, though she thought it could be rather awful. "Would you spell your names for me?" She dragged her notebook out of her shoulder bag as she asked.

"H-I-L-L," the woman said. "Just like the store, except there's an apostrophe and an 's' on the end—Hill's Office Supply. Hester and Avery."

"Have you always been in this same location?" Maxey asked, scribbling.

Mrs. Hill nodded. "Always."

"What did you think when you heard there'd been a fire right next door?"

"I thought, 'Oh, lord, if Avery didn't pay that last insurance premium, I'm going to kill him.'" Her laugh sounded strictly social, without any real pleasure behind it.

The front door rattled open. The gentleman who came through it was gray—cap, hair, topcoat, slacks, boots. Even his skin had the ashy color of someone with bad circulation. A white bakery bag drooped from one hand.

"Avery." Mrs. Hill motioned for him to hurry up, which had no effect whatsoever on his plodding gait. "This lady is from the newspaper. Tell her something about Derrick's fire and you'll get some free publicity for us."

"Don't know anything about the fire." He scuffed to a full stop and held up the bag. "They were out of raspberry." Half a head taller than his wife, his eyes magnified by rimless glasses, he had the air of someone rarely moved to laughter.

"When did you know there was a fire next door to you?" Maxey forged on, still hoping for one zinger remark she could quote.

Mrs. Hill put her hands on her hips. "Not till the next morning when we came to open up. Can you believe that? You'd think someone would have known we'd want to know."

"Wasn't anything we could do," Avery Hill said. "Might as well get our sleep."

"Did it do any damage to your side of the building?"

Mr. Hill shook his head.

Mrs. Hill snorted. "Stunk up the place to holy hell. We've had the back door open ever since, but the smell has settled in the ceiling tiles and the floorboards. It'd cost a fortune to get it all cleaned up. I could just—Derrick should never have let that drifter spend the night. Dumb kids." Her blue eyes suddenly glittered with tears, and she turned away, searching her tunic pocket for a handkerchief.

The phone rang at the check-out counter in the center of the room. Mrs. Hill rushed to answer and then seemed to be taking an order for delivery. Mr. Hill wandered toward the back with his donuts.

Maxey browsed the pen department, choosing an assortment of inexpensive rolling writers for herself and an orange-barreled Denver Broncos ballpoint for Scotty. She carried them to the cash register, where Mrs. Hill was just telling her telephone customer to have a nice day.

"I'll give you a ten per cent business discount," Mrs. Hill said, ringing up Maxey's purchase. "Oh. Hear that? Derrick's here."

"That" was a thumping beat like a giant heart. Derrick's Muzak was apparently a cranked-up stereo playing rock, the bass percussion reverberating through the walls.

Maxey accepted her change from Mrs. Hill's arthritis-gnarled fingers. "Would you be interested in an ad in the *Regard* some time?"

"Oh, honey, we have more business than we want already. We keep five full time employees hopping—six in the winter months."

"That's great."

"It is when you consider all the competition from the new cut-rate, cut-throat discount stores."

"Oh, uh-huh." Maxey felt a flush of guilt. She usually bought her office supplies at K-Mart.

Mrs. Hill slammed the cash register, making the coins jangle. "So-called superstores taking over everything—drugstores, bookstores, hardware stores, office supply stores—killing us moms and pops. Free enterprise is going down for the third time."

Thud, thud, thud. Derrick Sikes' background music pounded like a headache.

"Thanks again," Maxey said, and followed her ears next door.

The Futon Lode's aroma rushed out to greet her—burnt feathers and scorched rubber.

A man walked toward her from the back of the store. "Hello! Everything's half off today. What can I sell you?"

Maxey couldn't imagine buying anything that would make her apartment smell like this, not even for one hundred per cent off. Derrick ought to take whatever insurance payment he could get and run.

"Are you Mr. Sikes?" she asked, wishing he'd turn down the music so she didn't have to yell.

"Derrick, yes." He smiled expectantly, as if strangers asking for him by name were no problem. That probably meant he paid his bills on time and kept his personal promises.

Maxey guessed his age at about twenty-seven or -eight. The first thing anyone would notice was his shoulder-length blond hair. The thick, gleaming-clean curls framed his long, thin face like a lion's mane on a pale gazelle.

Maxey identified herself and her reason for being there. "Is there anything you'd like to say about Basil Underwood?"

Derrick looked down at the pointy toes of his blue

lizard cowboy boots. "Just that I didn't know him very well, but I sure do hate the day he took up smoking. I thought I was doing the guy a favor, but I'd have been kinder to tell him to bug off, find somewhere else to crash for the night. Excuse me a minute."

He whipped around and strode toward the back. Maxey couldn't help staring at his narrow bottom in what looked like shrink-wrapped blue jeans. He disappeared through a door on the right. After a moment, the drums and guitars shut off in mid-quake.

Maxey wandered that direction, along an aisle surrounded by futons in rows, like a military barracks except for the pink stripes, red florals and purple plaids of the fabrics.

Derrick emerged from his office. "I suppose you want to see the fire scene?"

"May I?"

He led her all the way to the back, through a double doorway equipped with two useless flaps like a stereotypical saloon's, into a large, open space that had once been an unfinished area for shipping/receiving. Now it lay as bleak and black as an empty coal bin. A new, silvery-steel back door stood open to the sunny alley, but Maxey's eyes still stung with the miasma of old smoke.

"How long had you known Mr. Underwood?" she asked.

"We went to high school together. Never hung out much, though. After graduation, we'd run into each other every now and then, have a drink or something. When he showed up—that night—I hadn't seen him for quite a while, maybe a year. He never had a lot of ambition, no big career. Hand to mouth—you know the type. Never married that I know of. No kids. That I know of."

"Parents? Siblings? Good friends?"

"I guess if he'd had any good friends, he'd have bummed a place to stay off of them instead of me. His folks were divorced, I think. No brothers. One sister that he used to fight with all the time. I mean really fight—they'd punch each other out, bloody noses." Derrick shrugged his thin shoulders. "Basil wasn't what you'd call, you know, happy."

Maxey stared at the floor and shook her head, the way people do when they feel sorry for someone else and blessed for themselves. The concrete floor gleamed black with char.

"How about you?" she asked. "How long have you been in the futon business?"

"About four years. Before that I worked at the X Emporium selling smut. I saw a lot more of ol' Basil then. I guess you don't want to mention his magazine collection in his obituary though." He laughed.

Maxey walked to the open door, ostensibly to peer out into the alley, actually to draw a breath of fresh air. "Do you run this place all by yourself?"

"I got a kid who handles the deliveries. My wife Torry does the bookkeeping."

"I won't take up any more of your time. Thanks for talking with me. I'll just slip out the back way here."

"You want to see a picture of Basil?"

Her foot on the sill, Maxey longed to step into the sunshine, but of course Derrick's words sucked her back like gravity into the black hole. "Sure."

He ushered her to his office, a walnut-paneled ten by ten space furnished with a gray metal desk, two gray metal folding chairs, and a brass-framed futon with a lambskin slipcover. Derrick went straight to the desk and picked up a book already lying open flat.

"High school year book." He pointed to one of the heads on a page of individual portraits. Derrick's fingernail needed cutting.

Maxey studied Basil Underwood. From below the Beatles hair-cut, he stared gravely into the camera. Not a bad-looking guy, if you didn't mind too much eyebrows and not enough chin.

"Here," Derrick said, taking the book back. "Here's his sister." He riffled pages, found one, presented it to Maxey.

She'd expected a big girl with heavy features, as would befit a pugilist. Derrick's over-long nail indicated a delicate-faced gamin with a short, shaggy haircut. Betsy Underwood, it said underneath.

"Does she live around here?"

"Never married and still lives with her mother, I think. She's probably in the phone book."

"I appreciate all your help." Maxey moved out into the showroom and turned aside to cough.

"Does it smell bad in here to you?" Derrick asked earnestly.

Maxey was about to laugh until she saw his serious face. "Don't you think so?"

"I've got anosmia. I can't smell anything, not since I was a kid and conked my head on the curb in a bike wreck."

"Wow. Well, yes, it does smell really bad in here. I don't think you're going to sell any of these futons."

"That's what Torry says. I didn't think it would hurt to try."

"Derrick, the only customer who might buy one of these mattresses is someone else with anosmia."

"Damn. That's exactly what Torry said."

He walked her to the front door.

"Change of subject." Maxey paused with her hand on the brass latch. "Did Sylvia Wellman ever come in here? You might have known her as Packy."

"Oh, yeah, her. She's in here all the time."

"She won't be any more. She died earlier this week."

"No kidding. Of natural causes?"

"Yes." Maxey squinted at him. "Why would you ask that?"

"Just 'cause she seemed to be so alone and vulnerable, you know? The weak zebra separated from the herd."

"Gosh, what a great metaphor. Mind if I use it when I write about her?"

He shrugged. "Feel free. I offered her five bucks once to wash the front window. Because I was feeling sorry for her, see, and the window needed it. She looked at me like I'd propositioned her for sex, shocked as hell. She walked out and didn't come back for about a month. I figured if I really wanted to keep her out of the store, I could just offer her another job. But I didn't mind her wandering in every now and then. Sometimes she'd be the only so-called customer I had all day. She'd go straight to the little table over there where I keep my sales literature, pick herself out a brochure, deposit it in her grocery sack, walk out, and never let slip a 'so long' or 'thank you'. Strange old bird."

"Zebra," Maxey corrected him. "So long and thank you, Derrick."

The perfume of Scotty's freshly made coffee welcomed Maxey to the office. She slung her shoulder bag into her desk drawer and snapped on her computer screen before crossing the room to draw a cup.

Meanwhile, Scotty typed as if the keys were hot potatoes, having grunted a greeting without glancing up. Maxey patted his hunched back as she returned to her own desk.

She hefted the Boulder telephone book out of its stack tray and flipped to the U's. There were five Underwoods listed, none of them Betsy, but one of them B. J. Holding the place with her forefinger, Maxey dialed the number.

"'Lo?"

"Ms. Underwood?"

"Yes?" The voice was raw, deep, and tired-sounding.

"This is Maxey Burnell. I'm looking for the sister or the mother of Basil Underwood."

There was a moment of silence. "Why?"

"I'm writing an obituary for my newspaper. I'd like to include anything you'd care to tell me about—your son, is it?"

"My son," the voice agreed. A silence settled.

"Mrs. Underwood? What was Basil doing recently? Where did he work?"

"He was between jobs."

"Uh-huh. Where did he work last?"

"I think he was out at IBM."

"International Business Machines? That IBM? Doing what?"

"Engineer. Something to do with computers."

"No kid—uh—where did he get his degree?"

"Degree?"

"His education. To be a computer engineer."

"Oh. Colorado."

"Colorado University?"

A heavy sigh was followed by more silence.

"Mrs. Underwood? Is Betsy there?"

"You mean B. J.?"

"Is B. J.'s full name Betsy?"

"Yes, but she hates that."

"All right. Is B. J. there? Could I talk to her?"

"No. She's sleeping."

"When would be a good time for me to reach her?"

Maxey listened to Mrs. Underwood breathe three whistling breaths. Then the line clanked and the dial tone kicked in.

"Damnation." Maxey hung up the receiver and checked her watch. She needed to apply her posterior to the seat of her chair and get some blankety-blank writing done.

"Sounded like a tough interview," Scotty remarked without turning around or perceptibly slowing his fingers.

"Worse. I don't think I can use any of it without confirmation. It didn't jibe with the profile I'd already been given of Basil Underwood." She flipped pages in the phone book again, retrieved the phone and dialed again.

"IBM. How may I direct your call?"

"Personnel, please."

"Thank you" was followed by one discreet ring.

"Personnel. Anderson."

Maxey told him the who, where, what, and why of her call.

"I'm sorry. It's not our policy to give out information

on the phone. We require that you put your request in writing on company letterhead."

"I'm on a deadline here. I'm writing an obituary. All I want to know is whether Basil Underwood was, in fact, an employee of IBM."

"If you'll fax your request, I'll try to fax the answer no later than tomorrow."

"Okay. Thanks."

She didn't bother to ask for the fax number. There was more than one way to skin a corporation.

She dialed the switchboard again, and when the same cool voice asked how to direct her call, Maxey asked for Basil Underwood.

There was a moment of silence as the woman searched the data bank, presumably. "Do you know what department he is in?"

"Sorry. Something to do with computers." The operator was too well-trained to laugh. After another few moments, she said she was unable to locate a Basil Underwood.

Maxey tossed her pen onto the desk. "Well, thanks anyway."

"Do you know his middle initial?"

Maxey blinked. Was the woman coaching her toward a correct answer? One in twenty-six was pretty favorable odds.

"J," Maxey said firmly. "B. J."

"Just a moment. I'll connect you."

A brusque male voice answered immediately. "Doug Niles."

"Hello. I'd like to speak to B. J. Underwood."

"Not here. Take a message?"

"I'm not sure. I'm not sure I have the right B. J. Underwood. Does B. J. stand for Betsy something?"

"Jeez, I hope not. I've never heard him called anything but B. J."

"How about Basil?"

"Well, that's better than Betsy. But I still haven't heard

him called anything but B. J."

"You asked if you could take a message. Does that mean you think he'll be in soon? That he's—" Maxey squirmed in her chair, not knowing how else to phrase it. "—Alive?"

"Man, what a weird conversation. B. J. is a real quiet guy, but far as I could tell, last time I saw him, he was still breathing."

"And when was that?"

"Last night."

"Last night." Maxey shook her head.

"Yeah. We were running some diagnostics. I went home. He stayed."

Curiouser and curiouser. "I guess I must have the wrong person. Is B. J. in his thirties? Dark eyebrows? Not a lot of chin?"

Doug Niles huffed a considering sigh into the receiver. "I guess that's not too bad a description."

"Look, I have a home phone number for the Underwood I'm trying to reach. Could you please check if it matches B. J.'s?" She read it off.

"Hang on a sec." He put her on hold.

Maxey sipped at her tepid coffee and listened to a tepid rendition of *Greensleeves*. Scotty yanked a page out of the printer, added it to the impressive stack he'd accumulated, and smartly rapped them on the desk top. He was probably done with his share of tomorrow's news, while Maxey was still spinning her wheels.

"Same number," Doug said.

She thanked him for his trouble and disconnected. Scotty had walked back to the restroom. In the quiet office, Maxey felt a stab of deadline panic. She still didn't know who Sylvia was, and now—who the hell was Basil?

4

While Scotty worked on page layout, Maxey composed her two stories. The one on Basil became an editorial on the apparent death wish of cigarette smokers. She would write a real obituary once she'd straightened out the facts on him.

The article on Sylvia took longer. By the time Maxey had rewritten the last paragraph four times, Scotty was pacing the floor, jacket and hat on, the folder full of tomorrow's *Regard* clenched under his left elbow.

"I saved you space on page three. Need any filler?" he asked as she heaved a satisfied sigh and leaned back in her chair.

"Give me a minute. I think I'm okay if we put a public service announcement in one corner. I wish I had a photo of Sylvia."

She rummaged in the computer, looking for an advertisement the right size, and settled on The Seven Warning Signs Of Cancer.

"A mite overkill, don't you think?" Scotty said across her shoulder. "Right after your sermon on cigarettes?"

"Nobody's going to read anything on this page anyway except maybe the first paragraph about Sylvia to see if she's someone they knew and what she died of."

"God, Maxey, I'm glad you don't write the way you talk. Come on, come on, come on. The Bronco's in the alley with the motor running. If I don't hit any red lights or funerals, I can have us at the printers in record time."

Hitting the print key, Maxey checked her watch. "Are you sure?"

"No question. Record time late."

But it was Maxey who took the *Regard* and the Bronco, because she wanted to stop at the Underwood house on the way back, and maybe catch the mysterious B.J. awake.

After she rushed out, the office seemed to sigh and relax. Scotty did, anyway. He wandered to the front door and looked out at the pedestrians flowing both ways on the promenade. A young man had set up a xylophone on the edge of the grass median, and the soft, bonging notes of *Ebbtide* struck Scotty with a momentary pang of nostalgia. He had been in Texas when that song was popular, not too old and not too young, independent as a hog on ice, as the saying goes. Different lady on his arm every Saturday night. Some of them on more than his arm. Talk about the good old days! Ah well, what was it Sandberg said? *History is a bucket of ashes*.

Scotty turned away from the door. He'd never been one to waste time. Or spin his wheels too long in one rut. It would be interesting to know where he'd be a couple of years from now. He doubted he could stand the hurry-up-and-wait news routine any longer than that—he was seventy-two, for Christ sake. Seventy-two!

Then again, he hated to think of the tears when he announced his decision to move on. Not all of them would be Maxey's.

He went to the restroom, and when he came back, there was a man hopping up and down beside Maxey's desk.

"Help you?" Scotty asked, realizing the hopping was in time to the xylophonist's snappy rendition of *Happy Days Are Here Again.*

Smiling unselfconsciously, the stranger bounced to a full stop and shoved out a big hand to be shaken. "Roberto Trueblood to see Maxey Burnell."

"Afraid she isn't here." Scotty stepped into the handshake and smelled mothballs. Roberto's black sweater had been washed with something white and linty. "Could I take a message?"

"I'll wait. Okay if I sit down?" He did before Scotty could say no. He swung Maxey's chair back and forth in slow half-circles.

Damn. If Roberto hadn't come in, Scotty could have put his head on his arms on the desk and taken a snooze. Now he had to look busy, to discourage the monologue this fidgety guy looked ready to uncork. Scotty lifted a handful of mail from the in-tray and sorted it into piles of his and hers.

"Nice little office," Roberto observed. "You could use some potted plants, though. They give off oxygen, you know. Help you think better."

"Mm-hm." Scotty frowned with exaggerated concentration at a red, white, and blue envelope. *Open Immediately!* it proclaimed. He hated bossy mail, especially when it arrived on a bulk rate stamp.

Roberto drummed his fingers on Maxey's desktop in time with the musical hammering outside. After a moment, he tilted back and gazed at the ceiling.

"You ought to get rid of these fluorescent lights. They cause cancer, you know."

Scotty pitched the junk mail at the wastebasket and missed. Roberto scrambled out of the chair in a show of helpfulness, picking it up and dropping it in. Then he strolled around the room inspecting everything. When he circled back to Maxey's desk, he leaned to look at her calendar.

"I'm not sure when she'll be back," Scotty said, expecting Roberto next to haul open drawers and stir through them. "Maybe you'd better catch her another day."

Roberto sat down again and hunched forward, hands on knees. "Is she good to work for?"

Startled, Scotty looked directly at him.

"I mean, she doesn't seem like a witch, but a lot of businesswomen are. And it can't be easy for an old guy like you to take orders from a young female, you know?"

Scotty's smile felt pasted on. "She doesn't order me around. We're partners."

"Ohh, uh-huh." Roberto cast another appraising look around the room. "How much did it cost you to go into this business?"

"Look, son, I'm going to have to ask you to leave a message and move on, so I can get some work done here."

"Well, sure. I didn't realize at first that you were a partner. I can deal with you instead of Maxey." Roberto lifted the front of his sweater and wrested out a yellow legal pad. "Maxey said to bring in my poetry. She's going to pick her favorites to run in the paper."

"Are you sure? The *Regard* doesn't publish—"

"Tell her to excuse the handwriting, but my typing is way worse." Roberto smoothed out the top sheet of paper and shoved the pad at Scotty.

"I'll pass this along." Scotty frowned at the backward-slanting cursive rendered in blobby ballpoint pen. "But I really wouldn't count on—"

"I don't expect any money, but I'll need a couple of tear sheets. Maxey knows my address."

"Phone number?" Scotty asked, giving up the fight.

"Oh, yeah, here." Roberto picked up a pen from Maxey's desk and scribbled on the white strip at the top of the pad. "This is a public phone, so don't be surprised if I don't get the message."

Taking back the pad and pen, Scotty stood up to herd Roberto toward the front door and open it wide for him.

"Tell Maxey I've got this friend who could do some great illustrations." Roberto smiled and squeezed Scotty's shoulder, letting go before Scotty could shrug away the patronizing gesture. Roberto raised his voice above the music and an overhead jet. "And tell Maxey I've got more poems. Lots more."

He loped off without a backward glance.

Scotty waited for a trio of young women in CU sweatshirts and cut-off jeans to chatter past him. Then he crossed to the xylophone player's brown fedora, yawning wide on the sidewalk. Fingering two dollar bills out of his wallet, Scotty dropped them into the hat.

"Play *Ebbtide* again," he said.

The address for the Underwoods was in the south end of Boulder near the Turnpike to Denver. The subdivision would have been new and promising in the fifties; in the nineties it looked old and disillusioned. Little dry yards fronted one-story houses with roofless concrete slab porches. The lawn ornaments outnumbered the trees.

Maxey nosed her Toyota in at the curb in front of a house in mid-block. She couldn't see a number, but according to the neighbors' numbers on either side, this had to be the place she wanted. The one-car garage door was clamped shut, as were the front door and all the white-blinded windows.

Sighing for the time she was probably wasting, Maxey got out of the car and went to ring the bell.

Seconds ticked by while nothing happened. Maxey punched the button again before turning away. She sensed, rather than heard, movement in the house, but when she depressed the button a third time, nothing stirred.

Back in the car, she was twisting the key in the ignition when a dusty black convertible with a scabby top zipped into the driveway and rocked to a stop. Maxey watched a man get out and reach back inside for two brown bags of groceries.

"Excuse me," she called, half in, half out of the Toyota. "I'm looking for B. J. Underwood."

"What do you want with him?"

The man watched her walk over, the grocery bags braced against his chest. A sudden sweep of wind lifted his shaggy brown hair and plastered his tan slacks to his beefy legs. He was a lot bigger below the waist than above, like a half-inflated balloon.

"Who are you?" he asked, and she thought her answer might determine whether he knew B. J. Underwood or not.

"Maxey Burnell," she said truthfully. "I knew Basil," she lied.

"Oh." He thought a moment. "I'm B. J." His voice reminded her of Rod Stewart's, low and husky.

"I phoned earlier, to get a statement for Basil's obituary in my newspaper, but Mrs. Underwood wasn't too—she couldn't answer my questions."

"Okay." He waited. His red lumberjack shirt, tasseled loafers, and four o'clock shadow didn't adhere to regulation IBM uniform. He wasn't on his way to work.

"I have to admit I'm perplexed. Basil's mother said he worked as a computer engineer at IBM."

"No. I do."

"Where did he work then?"

"Hardly anywhere, I'm afraid. He had a reputation for hiring on at minimum wage jobs and quitting as soon as he accumulated some minimum living expenses. Also, he sponged off his mom."

"Uh-huh. He never married? No kids?"

B. J. shook his head.

"Hobbies? Honors?"

B. J. shrugged.

"And where's his sister Betsy?"

B. J. sighed. "Dead."

"Dead! What happened?"

"Car accident. In California. About five years ago."

"What a shame. But Mrs. Underwood said Betsy was asleep when I phoned this morning. In fact, from what she said, I thought B. J. was Betsy."

"Lenora is easily confused. She's harmless, but she's not what you'd call of sound mind."

Reflexively, Maxey glanced at the house in time to see a window blind twitch back into place. "So what's your relationship to the family, B. J.?"

"I'm a cousin. Lenora's husband's brother's son."

Maxey raised one finger to indicate she was sorting it out. Nodding, she smiled. "Did you grow up in Boulder, too?"

"No, California."

"How'd you end up here?"

He jiggled the groceries higher against his chest. "When Betsy died she was on vacation, visiting us, and I took charge of the funeral arrangements, getting the body home and all. Lenora seemed so fragile, I stuck around to help her over the worst, but the worst never seemed to get any better, so I just stayed."

"I can see a family resemblance," Maxey said to explain her staring at his face, which was better-looking than the photo of Basil and better-looking than his co-worker's description of him. He had more chin and less eyebrows than she'd expected. She felt bad for B. J., that his physique didn't match his voice.

"My ice cream is melting," he said, smiling apologetically.

"Sorry. I do appreciate your sorting out the names for me." Maxey backed away, worrying, as usual, that she'd forgotten to ask a critical question. When she reached the car, she waved, and B. J. tossed his head back in acknowledgement before striding toward the house.

Maxey fumbled with her purse, her notebook, the radio, and her keys, stalling for a possible glimpse of Lenora Underwood when B.J. opened the front door. A glimpse was all she got—of a flowered muumuu the size of a small tent.

"I told him three versions of no," Maxey exclaimed, flinging her arms into the air. "The man has the sensitivity of a ball peen hammer and he claims he's a poet?"

Scotty studied the yellow legal pad which Maxey refused to touch. "Roberto is feeling mortal. Like Napoleon pointed out, 'Glory is fleeting, but obscurity is forever.'"

"Well, he isn't getting his fleeting glory in the *Regard.*

He can damn-well self-publish his alleged poetry."

"You haven't read any of this. Here. Let's just read a line or two. 'Sleeping, it suddenly was clear to me / that dreams are feelings that enthuse everybody / 'twixt their laying down and awaking into the new morning.'"

"No comment," Maxey commented. She rearranged the clutter on her desk.

Scotty tossed the pad aside. "It's four-twenty. How about we blow out the lights and straggle home?"

"You go on. I'm staying awhile."

"Didn't H. G. Wells say that on his death bed?"

Maxey laughed, and as he started shutting off the overhead lights, she grabbed up her purse and beat him to the door.

The next day was a typical Thursday. Quiet. A time to clean up the office after the past week's edition, and take a few deep breaths before beginning on the next week's edition. Scotty called it, "Pushing in all the stops."

Maxey often wondered, in these calms between storms, what she'd be doing today if she hadn't inherited the newspaper from Jim Donovan. Probably her favorite memory of Jim was seeing him for the first time, the day she walked in off the promenade, looking for a job and not really expecting to find one at such a little operation as *The Blatant Regard.*

She had on a navy dress and white heels and felt overdressed the minute she stepped into the cramped, messy office. Before her eyes adjusted completely to the dimmer light, she heard a call for help. It wasn't urgent enough to scare her, but it definitely surprised her to discover the big man who'd issued it.

"Boy, am I glad to see you," he'd bellowed. He stood at an odd, hunched angle at a desk across the room, peering over his shoulder at her. "I got a little problem here."

Hoping he wasn't a pervert, she sidled closer.

"There's a pair of scissors over there in that pencil cup.

Cut me loose, will you?"

His T-shirt tail was caught in the platen of his computer printer.

Whether he hired her out of gratitude for her help (and her future silence about his ineptitude), or because he liked her modest credentials (a few semesters of college and five years with her Ohio hometown newspaper, mostly baby-sitting the editor's kids)—he did hire her.

And was her friend for too short a time before he died and left the newspaper to her and her ex-husband.

She had no idea where she'd be working if not here, but she liked this job just fine, especially now that she had Scotty to share the burden and the joy. She didn't kid herself that he'd stick around long. But she had plenty of experience with being left behind by men she cared for, and she'd survive Scotty's leaving, too.

Now she looked up from filing paid receipts, remembering one of those self-help books she'd checked out of the library and tried to read until it got way too Pollyanna for her. She did recall, *Live for the moment. Enjoy the moment you're in.*

"Love the one you're with," she said out loud.

"Uhh?" Scotty, slouched in his swivel chair, one foot propped on his desk, frowned at the list—probably grocery—he was making.

Maxey let the file drawer roll shut. "Let's lock the door and go someplace really nice for lunch. My treat."

"The deli's really nice."

"Yeah, but I mean with four-page menus, soft benches, Muzak."

"Oh. You mean expensive."

"We'll exchange ten words about the office telephone bill and call it a business meeting—tax deductible."

"In that case—" Scotty stood up and smoothed at his hair to get ready. "Let's go to The Broker and get all the deductibles we can eat."

***

From the October 27th *Blatant Regard:*

FAMILIAR PEARL STREET FIGURE DIES

Sylvia Wellman spent her nights in a one-room apartment in the Bluebell House and her days walking the streets of Boulder, mining treasure that no one else could see. Few people knew her real name, but many knew "Packy," because of her avid collecting—matchbooks, brochures, toothpicks, business cards, whatever was free and captured her fancy. She saved her favorites in two plastic boxes—one bright red, one cheerful yellow.

On Wednesday, October 23rd, Sylvia fell down a flight of steps at the Bluebell, breaking her hip. Two days later, pneumonia moved in. Two days after that, it killed her.

Kent Lawson, the manager of Sunglass Connection, was sorry to hear of her death. "Packy worried me when she first started stopping in," he said. "I thought she was going to rip off stock if I turned my back. Pretty soon I relaxed. She didn't want shades. She wanted the little give-away packets of cleaner with our name on. She never took more than one per visit. Sometimes she'd leave me a paper clip or a penny in exchange. I'll kind of miss her coming in."

Other Pearl Street merchants feel much the same way. Jeanette Newsom of Off Broadway Arts called Sylvia "a harmless sourdough prospecting for junk." Morrie Lutz, the owner of Dilly Deli, saw her as a woman with a grail complex, and also considered her harmless. The Futon Lode's Derrick Sikes compared her to a weak zebra cut off from the rest of the herd. He didn't mind her occasionally finding refuge in his store.

Not all businesses could be so charitable, however. Sylvia was not welcome at many of the restaurants along the mall. Managers and owners felt she was bad for business, disturbing their customers. One such restaurateur commented that, "She didn't smell bad, but she looked like she did, so we had to discourage her coming in."

Sylvia's past is as mysterious as she herself. Where did she come from? How did she make a living? Who and where were her family?

She was buried this week without ceremony, without friends or relatives in attendance. Probably she wouldn't have wanted any of these. Probably she would have been happy to know that the wind dropped one gray feather on her casket.

"I don't know. Maybe it's too sentimental. Is it too sentimental?" Maxey asked Calen.

They sat hip to hip at her kitchen table, demolishing a pepperoni pizza, the day's *Regard* spread like a tablecloth under their elbows.

"No. It's great." Before she could feel reassured, he added, "Besides, you had to write it in a hurry."

"I have to write everything in a hurry. That's my job description—collect the facts and type like hell. So you don't like it? Damn. I wanted it to be special for Sylvia."

"No, no. I said it was great. Let's go to a movie."

"Don't you want to just rent a video?"

"Let's do a real movie for a change. See something while it's still hot." He playfully bumped against her, making her miss her mouth with the last bite of pizza.

Wiping her cheek with the back of her hand, she nodded. "Okay. But nothing too serious. Not a heart-warming tear-jerker."

"Right," he said, grinning as he pushed back his chair. "Not sentimental."

Three hours later, Maxey congratulated Calen for finding a parking space almost in front of her place after circling the block only ten times, and they walked up the dark street, both of them mellow and sleepy.

"What's going on that there's so much traffic?" Calen asked, twining his left fingers through Maxey's right fingers. "It's too late an hour for a yard sale."

"Parties, I guess. Boulder loves its Halloween season."

"Did you like the movie?"

"It was okay. Too salty."

"Salty?"

"I prefer my popcorn with a little salt and a lot of butter."

"Ever notice how your house sort of looms out over the sidewalk?"

"It's not my house."

"Fall of the house of Burnell. A family legacy brought down by evil from within." He hummed a few notes of ominous soundtrack.

"The only evil within," Maxey said, "is a pound bar of milk chocolate I hid from you, two overdue library books, and Moe's litter box." She linked arms with Calen and hauled him up the front steps. "Move it, Taylor. Hurry up before a vampire gets us." She let him go so she could search the key out of her shoulder bag.

He yawned and rubbed his knuckles into his eyes. "Nope, we're safe. It was just a movie. And a novel before that. There's no such thing as—"

Maxey's horrified gasp cut him off. Recoiling from her front door, she stepped hard on his toe. "Look at that!"

The wooden frame beside the knob looked like a bear had swatted it. The door itself hung open half an inch, a sly invitation to slip inside.

"We can call the police from my mobile phone," Calen said, pulling her by her sleeve.

"No, wait. Let's check the door at the top of the steps. If it's locked, we'll know they didn't make it all the way inside."

"Maxey, believe me, the police won't mind dropping by to look at this, even if there's no other evidence of felony. Come on. You don't want to be on the stairs if the guy is up there determined to come down."

She let him shepherd her off the porch. While he leaned into the station wagon to make the phone call, she crossed the street to get far enough away for an unobstructed look at her bedroom windows. They were closed and dark except for the reflection of a street lamp. No light shone in Ollie Kraig's downstairs windows. She checked her watch. Almost midnight.

Calen backed out of the wagon and quietly clicked the door shut. Maxey strolled over to lean against a front fender with him. Now and then a car growled past, but mostly the block stretched tranquil, oblivious to whatever crime had occurred here or might be occurring elsewhere in town.

In fewer than five minutes, a dark and silent patrol car eased in at the curb in front of them, and the driver shouldered out. He flashed a light in their faces just long enough to see they were unarmed and not dangerous.

"You the party that phoned about a break-in?"

"Right. This is Maxey Burnell, and it's her apartment. I'm Calen Taylor of the Boulder Fire Department. Do I know you, officer?"

"Sure. Emilio Madrid."

The men shook hands. Maxey felt a sweep of relief that responsibility for the situation now lay on Madrid's broad shoulders. She was glad Calen hadn't let her go upstairs. Looking for monsters in the closets and under the bed wouldn't have been anywhere near as much fun as watching them on the giant screen.

They trooped up on the porch to examine the forced door in the light of Madrid's torch. Motioning them to stand back, he nudged the door a bit wider and shone the light up the stairs.

"I've got backup on the way. Better wait for it. Is there a rear entrance?"

Maxey shook her head before she realized he couldn't hear that. "No."

"Somebody live downstairs?"

"Yes, an elderly gentleman named Kraig."

"Is there an inside stairway from your place to his?"

"No."

Another patrol car slid up beside Madrid's, made a U-turn and parked across the street. Madrid went to confer with his colleague.

Maxey scrubbed at her arms, wishing for a heavier jacket, wondering if the burglar had left her one.

The two policemen split up, one walking toward the back through the side yard. Madrid stepped onto the porch, his radio quietly spitting communication between dispatch and some other crime scene.

"What's at the top of these steps?"

"Another door." Maxey fished in her pocket for the key. "You might need this. Sometimes I lock it and sometimes I don't, depending on where I'm going and whether I've been thinking about escalating crime." She stopped, afraid she was babbling, and started fresh. "The door leads to an open area with the kitchen on your left and the living room straight ahead and a bedroom and bathroom on the right."

"Okay. You folks wait in your car till we get this checked out." He shut off his radio, opened the door, and hand on holster, began to climb.

Calen hustled Maxey off to sit in the wagon. Unable to see her windows for the porch roof, she settled for watching the seconds count up on the dashboard digital clock.

When they'd flickered through four minutes' worth, Madrid reappeared on the porch and motioned to them.

Maxey sighed hard. "False alarm."

They followed Madrid up the echoing stairwell. "The door up here wasn't locked or tampered with," he said, handing back her key. "You check whether anything is missing."

The rooms still smelled faintly of pizza and coffee. Maxey looked around, trying to see her habitat as a stranger would see it—dishes in the sink, a plain wooden dinette set nearly buried under books and newspapers, a frowzy sofa and matching shabby chair, a framed photo of Longs Peak slightly askew on the wall, a well-worn carpet in shades of gold accented with gray cat hair.

"Looks good to me," she said.

"How about the bedroom?" Madrid prompted.

She and Calen surveyed the little room and closet and

adjoining bathroom. They both shrugged.

"All I see wrong is what an awful housekeeper I'm becoming." Maxey scooped up a handful of dirty clothes and stuffed them into the laundry basket.

"Looks like your intruder was scared off before he got this far. We'll talk to your neighbors, see if anyone heard or saw anything."

Maxey suddenly realized what was missing. "Moe!" She began a new, more urgent search at ground level. "Here, kitty, kitty, kitty."

He'd never before come when she called, so she didn't panic when he didn't come now. Dropping to hands and knees, she peered under the bed. Golden eyes peered back.

"You okay, sport?" she asked him, knowing better than to reach under and haul him out. He'd scratched her for lesser presumptions. He'd probably scooted into hiding when he heard Madrid's unfamiliar tread on the stairs.

"I guess we're all present and accounted for," she said, still kneeling. "Thank you for coming."

"If you need us again, give us a ring." Madrid switched on his radio to call in a code four, and Calen walked him to the door.

It wasn't till she wakened with the alarm clock the next morning that Maxey knew what the intruder had stolen. Padding straight to the three-shelf bookcase in the living room, she verified what her subconscious had perceived during the night. An empty space on the bottom shelf indicated where Sylvia Wellman's two plastic treasure boxes had been.

5

"Weird, huh?" Maxey said, dusting her computer screen with a damp paper towel.

"Yeah. Maybe one of the boxes had a false bottom full of securities," Scotty said, dusting his desk by leaning over and blowing on it. "Who knew you had Sylvia's stuff?"

"You and Calen. The lady at the hospital who gave one to me. Georgiana Flint, Robert Truet, and a bunch of guys hanging around the Bluebell House who saw me with the other one. I might have mentioned having the boxes to someone I was interviewing yesterday for the Sylvia story. I guess anyone could have inferred it from the story itself."

"That certainly narrows the suspects down." Scotty took out a folded white handkerchief and spanked the arms of his rolling chair. Housecleaning finished, he sat down and clasped his hands over his waist. "Find out why and you'll find out who did it."

"Or find out who and then know why," Maxey said, lifting the telephone receiver to swab the mouthpiece with her towel.

Hearing a squeak, she put it to her ear. "Hello?"

"Hello? I didn't hear it ring. Maybe I've got the wrong number. Is this the newspaper office?" The voice had the unmistakable quaver of an old man probably accustomed to dialing wrong numbers.

"This is Maxey Burnell at the *Regard* newspaper. May I help you?"

"You're the one wrote about Sylvia. Nice article."

He might be old, but he obviously had remained sharp. Maxey's smile warmed her voice. "Thank you. Did you know Sylvia?"

"Sure did. Neighbors the last few months. Since you're interested in her—sympathetic, I guess you'd say—I thought you'd maybe be interested in her favorite box. I hate to pitch it, but it's no good to me. And there's at least one item that might be good to somebody."

"Another box? Don't tell me she had more. You have a Sylvia box?"

Scotty swiveled his chair around to stare at Maxey. She shrugged extravagantly.

"A neon purple one. Ugly thing, full of junk." The man on the phone chuckled, and that segued into a cough.

"I'd like to see it," Maxey said when she thought he could hear her again. "Are you at the Bluebell?"

"Top floor. The name's Lloyd Roswald. Don't worry. I'll be here whenever you come."

"Damn," Maxey said after the thanks and goodbyes. "I hate to go over there again and maybe run into Robert Truet."

"Wear a fake nose and moustache."

"Can you believe it? Roswald calling right now when we're talking about Sylvia? If it wasn't for last night, I'd say forget it. But here's a chance to take another look at Sylvia's treasure. Maybe this box of Roswald's is the one the intruder really wanted."

"You won't be able to forget it if you don't take a look."

Maxey yanked open the desk drawer where she kept her shoulder bag. "Okay. I'm going now and get it over with."

"Let me fetch the box back here," Scotty said, getting to his feet.

"No, I'll do it."

"I can see you gritting your teeth."

She opened her mouth wide to show she wasn't. "I can't

let a creepy apartment building and a crummy poet keep me from my appointed rounds."

"Maxey, I'll go, and to pay me back, you can take my turn cleaning the restroom."

She hesitated.

"You can take my turn cleaning the restroom," Scotty said, "and take my turn phoning the delinquent accounts."

"The restroom's enough," Maxey said, dropping her bag back into the drawer and kneeing it shut.

Scotty had lived in places like this in his time. He hoped to God he never had to again. On the first floor, he passed an overflowing diaper pail outside a closed door, the stench of it enough to bring the memories flushing back, of a urine-scented hall leading to a room—Little Rock, it was—where he could have done a field study on cockroaches if he'd wanted to band their ugly little legs.

Maxey had drawn him a map of how to get to the top rooms, and he strode up stairs and along corridors as if daring anyone to look at him crossways.

Robert Truet's door, which she had marked on her map with a skull and crossbones, was tightly shut.

As he scuffed up the stairs to the third floor, someone shouted, "Told you and told you and told you!" A door crashed shut and silence rushed back. By the time Scotty reached the top, there was no sign or sound of anger.

He walked the length of the hall both ways, looking for some hint of which room might be Roswald's. Finally, mentally shrugging, he knocked at a random door.

The young man who answered had obviously breakfasted on something stronger than Wheaties. Scotty thought he could see an aura of alcohol fumes rising off the kid like wavering air around a gasoline can.

"Roswald?" Scotty asked.

The kid smiled beatifically, pointed across the hall, and slowly shut the door in Scotty's face.

Roswald surprised Scotty by answering before he'd finished knocking and by being enormous. Men shrink with age, so Roswald must have been eight feet tall as a youth. He wore navy sweatpants, a tattletale gray undershirt and brown slippers the size of life rafts. His face was as wrinkled as wadded paper and his head gleamed smooth and hairless as a doorknob. When his hand swallowed Scotty's in a firm but gentle clasp, Scotty experienced the disconcerting sensation of being a little boy again.

"Who'd you say you were?" Roswald asked, smiling, ready to be pleased whatever the answer might be.

"I didn't. Scotty Springer from the *Blatant Regard.* Maxey couldn't come for the box, so she sent me. I can show you some ID." He slapped the back pocket of his jeans, ready to pull out his wallet.

"No, no, no need. Will you sit down?" Roswald swept an arm toward the dining set at stage left. Scotty imagined he could feel the breeze this stirred.

"Can't stay, thanks. It was good of you to let us know about this box."

Roswald folded his arms and made no move to get it. "Pretty sorry stuff in it. There's a key, though. That might be interesting."

Scotty nodded. They both nodded. Scotty could see that Roswald wasn't eager to hand over the box and say goodbye. People who live alone usually don't get their minimum daily requirement of conversation.

Sighing, Scotty motioned at the table. "Could I sit down and look through the box?"

"Surely." Roswald leaped to haul out a chair and then strode to a battered leather trunk at the foot of his neatly made bed to lift out a purple plastic cigar box. "Here she is."

Scotty couldn't help counting the steps it took for the old man to recross the ten foot wide room. Two. He folded himself into the creaky chair next to Scotty's.

"Lloyd, you probably get tired of folks asking, but were you a basketball player?"

"Nope. Too tall." Roswald grinned and stuck out his

tongue, which was the texture and color of an overripe pork cutlet.

Scotty hastily began stirring through the box. With even greater haste, he jerked his hand away, staring at the largest, ugliest thing in it—a military green hand grenade.

"Realistic, isn't it?" Roswald picked it out of the box and kneaded it like a rubber ball.

Scotty breathed again before continuing his inventory: A Cross pen that seemed to have been run over, a cigarette, a two-inch length of bright red yarn, a brass washer, a politically incorrect "flesh" crayon, a cardboard bookmark advertising a romance novel. . . .

"The key," Roswald said, digging his finger into the box and scraping out the tiny metal cross.

"Oh, yeah," Scotty said, disappointed. It was the universal tin key that would fit any cheap briefcase or metal box. He pincered up a rhinestone button and examined it as if it were a diamond. "How long did you know Sylvia?"

"Not long. I've only been here six months."

"Didn't take you much time to become friends." Scotty motioned at the junk. "For her to trust you with this."

"I don't know about friends. What it was, was, she knew her property was safe with me. Something about my presence, don't you know."

Sensing that Roswald was about to stick out that tongue again, Scotty tipped his head to frown into the box. "Were you here the evening she fell?"

"Uh-huh."

"Did you hear or see anything unusual before she took the tumble?"

"Unusual, huh? Let me see. There was some screaming and crying and carrying on. Nothing unusual."

Remembering the shouts as he came upstairs, Scotty nodded. "Think it was an accident then?"

"Oh, is that what you're aiming at? Are we considering suicide here? Or maybe murder?" He dum-dee-dumed a quavery rendition of the *Twilight Zone* signature notes.

"Just asking." Scotty snapped the lid shut and hopped his chair back, getting ready to stand. "Thanks, Lloyd."

"Nope, I didn't play basketball. I did play football, though. I was a goal post." The old man laughed at his old joke so hard he choked. Eyes watering, he waved as Scotty escaped out the door with Sylvia's box.

Maxey swished the blue, sudsy water around the bowl and flushed it half a second after the front door banged. After tapping the brush against the rim, she leaned out into the main room to check who had come into the office. And groaned.

The irony was she'd stayed here swabbing out a toilet to avoid Robert at the Bluebell.

"Caught you at a bad time, huh?" he greeted her, grinning immoderately.

She put away the brush, washed her hands, blew her nose, and —still not ready—strolled out to meet him. She felt like a schoolmarm about to ruin a kid's weekend with an F.

"Actually, I'm glad you stopped by," she said. "I want to give you back—"

"Cujo did some sketches," he said, waving a file folder. He loped closer and spread it open.

Involuntarily, she glanced down at the page of manila drawing paper covered with delicate flowers and clever little animals. Hardening her heart, she aimed a cold stare at Robert's sparkling eyes.

"Very nice. I'm sorry I can't use them. As I told you, I can't use your poems. I want you to take them back." She fumbled around beside her on the desk, not looking away from him, determined that he should see how immovable she was on this. "I'm sure you're quite talented, but this newspaper does not publish poetry or fiction. Or nonfiction from outside sources," she hastened to add before he could anticipate anything in that direction. "You need to submit your work elsewhere. To some of the small press magazines, probably."

Locating the legal pad, she picked it up and thrust it at him. His smile faltered. When he didn't take the pad, she slapped it against his chest. The smile twisted into a wince. He took the pad.

He stared down at it. "You didn't like the topics. None of these was on the right subject, right?"

Maxey shrugged. "You could say that."

Robert yanked out Scotty's chair and bounced into it. "Tell me what subject you want and I'll write a poem about it." He reached in through the neck of his crew neck sweater and fished up a ballpoint pen.

"No, Robert." Maxey had never seen red before. It startled her to realize that anger really did affect the eyes like that. Blinking to clear the rosy fog, she stretched to get the telephone and drag it within dialing distance. "I have work to do and I want you to leave. If you don't go at once, I'm going to phone the police and complain of harassment."

Robert's mouth slowly pursed into a wordless "O". His face paled before it blazed. Jutting his jaw, he leaped from the chair, shoved it backwards into the desk, and stomped toward the door. Instead of slamming it after him, he left it wide open to the cheerful sounds of the mall.

After a full minute, when her hands and knees felt a fraction steadier, Maxey walked to the door and slammed it herself.

"I can see that it's Sylvia's favorite box," Maxey said, brushing heads with Scotty as they studied the contents he'd dumped out on his desk. "Why, she could've sent that pen back to Cross. They've got a lifetime guarantee, no questions asked. What's a little tire tread on the barrel?"

She lifted out a scrap of yellow, lined paper and unfolded it to find nothing on either side, not even, thank goodness, a bad poem.

"I still don't recognize anything that a person would want to burglarize your apartment to get."

"Something with sentimental value, maybe."

Scotty snorted. "The guy would have to have more nostalgia than a Woodstock alumnus, to risk going to jail for whatever Sylvia had."

Maxey stopped sorting through the pathetic little pile and leaned back in her chair. "I spilled one of the boxes on the stairs at the Bluebell, and I didn't pick up everything that fell out."

Scotty spread his hands, palms up. "There you go. That's where the winning lottery ticket went."

"You know what we could do? We could let everybody I talked to earlier know that we've got this other box. When the bad guy comes to steal it—freeze! We got him."

"You've been reading too many amateur sleuth paperbacks. You really want someone sneaking into your apartment again? Or this office?"

"I was thinking we could mention that the purple box is in the glove compartment of your Bronco."

"Very funny."

"Okay, so where should we put it?"

"How about over there beside the coffee pot?"

"Hide in plain sight? Isn't that a little too plain?"

"Damn right. So we don't have to clean up a big mess if someone breaks in here to search."

Maxey couldn't bring herself to simply set it on the table. She wedged it sideways in a row of reference books squeezed between gray metal bookends. The purple plastic stood out like a sore thumb and several fingers.

"Okay, what's first to do for the next *Regard*?" Scotty asked, scrubbing his hands together as if he could hardly wait.

"Do you mind holding the fort while I go out and get a few interviews?"

Scotty hauled out his lower desk drawer and lifted out a brown sack. "I can hold it down better if I add a little ballast. Leftover pizza, leftover tossed salad, leftover napkin," he said, setting each item on the desk top.

Bringing him a cup of leftover coffee, Maxey decided her first interview would be at the Dilly Deli.

"Mind if I share your table?"

Maxey looked up from the *People* magazine she'd been skimming through while she consumed her chicken salad sandwich. The lady from the office supply store smiled down at her, waiting for permission to sit. In the background, the deli bustled and buzzed with the lunch crowd.

"Please do," Maxey said, pulling her plate and iced tea glass closer to make room.

Mrs. Hill set her black patent handbag on the little round table, saw that wouldn't do, moved it to the seat of the extra chair, and sat down across from Maxey.

"You look familiar," Mrs. Hill said, fingering the brooch on her tweed suit lapel.

"I was in your store a few days ago. Maxey Burnell from the *Regard*."

Mrs. Hill blinked. She looked around the room as if searching for another vacant chair. In profile, her face appeared younger, the nose and chin strong and sharp, the visible ear delicate above a single pearl earring. She turned back to Maxey, and all the wrinkles seemed to fall into place.

"I'm not going to ask you to buy an ad," Maxey promised.

"Okay."

"Do you eat here often?"

"Usually I pack a lunch from home. Now and then I just have to get away or I'll scream. Eat at a restaurant, shop a bit, take a real lunch hour."

"I know the feeling. Sometimes I think I don't own my business, it owns me."

"Exactly!" Mrs. Hill hitched up straighter and stabbed the table with a forefinger. "Avery and I open and close every day, before any of our employees come in and after they've gone home. Including Sundays and the lying awake at night, we've devoted our lives to supplying others with pens and receipt books and cash register rolls. I wish I had a minute's peace for every paper clip I've sold."

"It could be worse, though. Your store is like my newspaper office—a nice, clean workplace and mostly nice, clean clients. And we do have roofs over our heads while we worry at night."

Mrs. Hill didn't seem to hear Maxey's uplifting message, continuing with her own down-dashing one. "We're getting too old for such a pace. Avery's had to do all the deliveries for the past week because our help's on vacation. Gone to Florida to play on the beach. *We* should be in Florida. All our friends went down there long ago."

Maxey tried to think of an inspirational response that might go over better than her last attempt. If Mrs. Hill hated the business so much, why didn't she sell it?

"We can't sell, you know," Mrs. Hill said.

Startled, Maxey nodded.

"We can't sell because of the superstores. Nobody wants to risk going up against them. Nobody's willing to work so hard for so little profit margin. We're stuck with the hot potato."

"I'm sorry."

"Me too." Mrs. Hill pouted her lower lip. "If I had my life to live over, I'd be a beautician. There's never going to be a cut-rate, serve-yourself warehouse where you get your tips frosted." Leaning back, she laughed uncertainly. "Sorry. I didn't mean to spoil your lunch."

"You didn't."

"Well, let's talk of something else."

"Do you have children?"

"Nope. Do you?"

"Nope."

They looked past each other's shoulders until Sondra brought Mrs. Hill the soup and salad she'd ordered. Then, between mouthfuls, she told Maxey a convoluted tale about Avery's running for city council in 1964 and why he didn't win and how that still adversely affected Boulder to this day.

***

Calen sat at the conference table with six of his colleagues, playing with his mechanical pencil, fighting to keep his eyes open, struggling to stay tuned to the incredibly dull discussion of fire department budget. He bit his cheek till it smarted, rubbed his eyes with both fists, and still felt snores backing up in his throat.

Maxey. He'd think about Maxey and his plans for her. That scared him enough to wake him a degree. They had met—what?—three years ago? Was that long enough? He'd known his wife Laura since they were in first grade, but it had turned out he hadn't known her at all. He'd thought she wanted kids, wanted homemaking, wanted a modest income and a quiet life; but those were only his desires that he bounced off her right back to himself like echoes off a barn. Meanwhile, Laura didn't know what she wanted, but she wanted *more*.

So she had hauled off and left him. And a few months later, Maxey had walked into his crime scene.

He'd been down in a basement, up to his boot-tops in the blackened debris, photographing the scene in hopes it would someday help convict an arsonist. From above and behind him came a cheery, very feminine voice. As he recalled, she said, "I'm Maxey Burnell from the *Regard*. May I ask you a few questions?" But she might just as well have said, "I'm Attila the Hun. Give me your wallet," and he'd have been just as quick to say, "Fine, sure, yeah."

It wasn't love at first sight, but he did like what he saw, a lot. And it was—stimulating—having her there in the noxious ruins with him, listening intently to his every word as he explained the clues he'd found and his interpretation of them. He couldn't remember smiling at her or being anything but his usual gruff, professional self. But she had smiled at him with the ease of someone used to doing it, and that night he thought of her briefly before he fell asleep thinking of char depths and burn patterns.

The next time he saw her—at another arson scene—he

probably did smile at her. And eventually he got up the nerve to ask her out to dinner. But matters really heated up—excuse the pun from a fireman—after she came home a year ago from a visit to her aunt in Nebraska. She'd gone for a few day's R and R, but she came back to Boulder knowing who had killed her mother a decade before. Still the happy young woman he'd begun to love, Maxey now seemed deeper, stronger. Calen thought she looked at him as if she were memorizing him for the future, having seen how undependable the present can be. It frightened him into worrying about the fragile good times himself. He made an effort at being bolder, inserting himself into her daily routine, making himself available for whatever and however much she wanted him to do. They never talked of marriage, but the possibility tantalized Calen, as strongly as sexual tension had teased him before their first night together.

Damn, he wished he could make up his mind. Wished he could ask Maxey and be confident of her yes.

He hadn't understood how to have and hold his wife. Was he any wiser about Maxey? Could he trust her with his life? That was all he needed—another alimony payment every month!

Once, in a moment of passion, Calen had called Maxey "Laura." Inwardly cursing himself, he struggled to apologize.

"It's okay," Maxey said, hauling him close again. "Just don't call me Max."

Remembering, he grinned, then literally wiped it off his face, before his fellow firemen could notice his daydreaming. He tuned in to their discussion just a minute too late.

"So what do you think, Calen?" his boss asked.

He blinked and surveyed the too-warm room full of familiar, worn faces.

"I think," he said truthfully, "I'm lost."

Maxey drifted the length of Pearl Street Mall, eddying into stores at random, fishing for new information on Sylvia, trolling for ideas for next week's stories. She netted nothing.

Arriving at the far east end, she decided to brave the waves of fast-moving traffic at Fifteenth Street and check on Derrick Sikes.

She found him fighting an uphill scrimmage, trying to convince two clean-cut young men that the futon they were reconnoitering would look and smell better in the privacy of their own home.

"Is there another futon store in Boulder?" one customer tactlessly whined.

"We'll think about it," the other man lied.

Neither one returned Maxey's smile as they brushed past her going out. Derrick's stereo played something full of drums and guitars that were definitely plugged.

"Sorry to interrupt," Maxey said.

"You didn't. They weren't serious." Derrick's brown leather pants hugged him as tightly as they'd once hugged the cow. His western shirt, loaded with silver rivets and pearlized buttons, glittered when he breathed. "I have made some sales in the last couple days though. Six." He grinned. "And only three of those futons came back."

"I want to get your reaction to something."

"Shoot."

"Do you know Basil Underwood's cousin, a guy named B. J. Underwood?"

Derrick shook his golden locks.

"He lives with Basil's mother. He says that Betsy was killed in an auto accident in California." Maxey watched Derrick think about it.

He shrugged. "Didn't know that. It's a shame. She was the smart one in the family. Always got all A's in science and math. Good at sports. Real cute, too, but she didn't seem to know it. Never dated much. Shy, I guess you'd say."

"Except when she was beating up on Basil?"

"Oh, yeah." Derrick whinnied a laugh. "She had a mean

left hook."

"Mrs. Underwood seemed really confused when I tried to talk to her. She first said that Betsy was asleep there at home."

"Huh. Bummer."

"Did Betsy hate her name when you knew her?"

"Didn't everybody hate their name in high school? Derrick— gag. I always wanted to be James. Jim Sikes. Doesn't that sound like *somebody*?"

Maxey, remembering her "call-me-by-my-middle-name-Diane" phase, had to chuckle. "So did you name one of your children Jim?"

"Torry wouldn't hear of it. Course, we have girls."

Still smiling, flapping a hand in farewell, Maxey stepped out into the quiet Colorado sunshine. Being privileged to be outside on such a beautiful day, she couldn't feel the afternoon had been wasted. And just because she'd been too cowardly to mention the purple box to anyone didn't mean she couldn't blab about it to the whole world in the next *Regard*. Feeling empowered, she turned north toward Spruce Street. She would pick up her car from in front of her apartment and drive over to interview Mrs. Underwood. Basil deserved a real obituary, and by God, Maxey would write it for him. And while she was at it, she would try to determine whether Betsy deserved an obituary, too.

6

Before getting into the Toyota, Maxey ran upstairs. Flipping open the phone book, she dragged a fingernail down to the name she wanted and punched the number into the dial. While it rang, she watched Moe wander out of the bedroom, his eyes blank from an interrupted nap.

"IBM," came crisply into her ear.

"B. J. Underwood, please."

After a moment's silence, the extension buzzed.

"Underwood," he blurted, as if this was an unwanted interruption.

"Sorry," Maxey said, putting extra alto in her voice. "Wrong extension."

She disconnected, feeling guilty, but also secure in the knowledge that the coast was clear at the Underwood residence. It was the sort of tactic that gave reporters a bad name. Maxey rationalized that if she was really without scruples, she'd have hung up on B. J. without apologizing.

The front stoop felt gritty underfoot. Maxey gave the doorbell another stab, suddenly remembering that Mrs. Underwood hadn't answered it the last time Maxey came calling. Well, hell.

She twitched around to look at the neighboring houses, all as quiet and closed as this one. A mailman in his summer blues—short trousers and black shoes and socks—came whistling up the street. He stepped up on the porch next door, clanked the metal lid on the wall-mounted box, and swung down and across the lawn toward Maxey.

"Morning," he said, hitching up his bulging canvas bag.

Maxey's shoulder ached in sympathy.

He reached past her to rap smartly on the storm door. "Doorbell doesn't work," he advised cheerfully. Stuffing a red flyer and a rolled magazine into the black box by the door frame, he strode away to the next stop on his appointed round.

The inner door in front of Maxey shuddered and swung inward. Mrs. Underwood peered through the dusty storm door window at her.

"Hello. I'm Maxey Burnell. We've talked on the phone. I'm still trying to write an obituary for your son. May I ask you a few questions?"

For a full thirty seconds, Mrs. Underwood stood considering it, her round, pale face as blank as milk. She lifted a stubby cigarette to her mouth, sucked, exhaled, tapped ash into her cupped hand. Then she jabbed the cigarette into her mouth and, squinting over the smoke, fumbled with the lock and pushed open the door.

"Thank you." Maxey stepped into the living room, a neat and gleaming showcase for the figurines, vases, pottery, and general bric-a-brac that crowded every vertical surface. A shadow box almost covered the far wall, displaying dollhouse articles too intricate for any child to touch.

"Sit down," Mrs. Underwood suggested. She herself waddled across the bare hardwood floor, picking up a pink, shell-shaped ashtray on her way to the sofa.

Maxey chose a Boston rocker with a pink and blue patchwork throw pillow against the back.

Basil's mother, like a little teapot, was short and extremely stout and every breath whistled in her throat. She dusted the ash from her hand into the shell and squirmed deeper into the sofa. Her caftan billowed around her, as white and wrinkled as a used bed sheet.

Maxey took notebook and pen from her shoulder bag and led off with something easy. "Basil was graduated from Boulder High School?"

"Yes."

"And what did he do after that?"

"Went to work at Pizza Pro."

"Uh-huh. And after that?"

Mrs. Underwood sighed smoke through her nose. "I don't remember."

"Did he attend college somewhere?"

"No."

"Did he work at IBM?"

"No."

Maxey lightly smacked her forehead. "I'm sorry. That's Betsy that worked at IBM."

"No." Mrs. Underwood sent Maxey a quick, annoyed look. "Betsy graduated Boulder High, went to CU, and died."

"Right. Whereabouts in California did that happen?"

"I don't know."

"When—"

"I don't know. Let's talk about Basil."

"Yes, of course." Maxey glanced around the fussy little room. "Do you have a photograph album? I'd love to see him when he was a little boy."

"Matter of fact—" It took Mrs. Underwood three tries to escape the sofa. Stubbing out the cigarette, she crossed to a closet beside the front door and stretched to draw out a red book from the overhead shelf.

Maxey moved over to sit beside her on the sofa. The pages, bound with black yarn, were cream-colored construction paper going brittle, the glue that held the photographs drying out and letting go. The photos had not been labeled as to who or where they were.

Mrs. Underwood seemed happy to be turning the pages, recalling when both her children were young and alive. The infants became toddlers became children became teens. The pages petered out with two graduation photos and no adult portraits.

Returning to a shot of an extended family get-together, the adults outnumbering the children, Maxey asked, "Who are all these people?"

Pleased, Mrs. Underwood pointed from face to face. "That's Basil, Betsy, me. That's Herb, Basil's and Betsy's father."

"He died—when?"

"About a year after I kicked him out. Alcoholic. That's Harvey, Herb's brother, and his wife Millie, and their two kids."

"Is it Harvey and Millie who live in California?"

"Yeah. This is Granny Schmidt, Millie's mother."

Maxey tapped the photograph. "Which of the kids is B. J.?"

"B. J.? No." Mrs. Underwood pointed. "That's Marvin, and that's Ronnie. Or is that Ronnie and that's Marvin?"

"Where's B. J. in this picture?"

Mrs. Underwood stroked the photograph. "He wasn't there that day."

"Have you got a picture of him when he was a kid?"

Mrs. Underwood turned pages slowly, her breath wheezing in and out.

A room away, the telephone rang.

"I'll get that," Mrs. Underwood said, struggling to her feet. She carried the album with her.

It seemed to take her forever to reach the phone. Whoever was calling seemed willing to wait. Maxey counted ten rings before Mrs. Underwood's muttered, "Hello?"

There followed a moment's silence. Slow, heavy footfalls marked Mrs. Underwood's progress back to the living room. She appeared with a portable phone, which she offered at arm's length to Maxey.

"It's for you."

"Me? Are you sure?" She hadn't told Scotty she was coming here.

She put the receiver to her ear. Static and the hum of an

engine wafted out. "Hello?"

"Ms. Burnell," B. J.'s distinctively husky voice addressed her. "I am now bearing left off the Diagonal Highway onto Foothills Parkway. I strongly suggest that you leave my aunt's house post haste and never, ever return."

Maxey cleared her throat so it wouldn't squeak. "Now, wait a minute—"

"Nuisance telephone calls, trespassing, harassment—I'm sure I could find something to interest the police. But I'd rather handle you myself. Believe me, you'd rather have the police."

"Are you threatening me?" Maxey blustered.

Unperturbed, Mrs. Underwood swayed from foot to foot, lighting another cigarette.

"How clever of you to notice," B. J. said. "Now I'm at the intersection of Foothills and Valmont. The light is green. Zooming through."

Maxey handed the phone to Mrs. Underwood. "We're finished talking." She stuffed her notebook into her bag and stood up. "Thank you for your time."

Mrs. Underwood, juggling phone, photo album, and cigarette, shuffled her feet till she'd turned around to face the door. Maxey pictured B.J. sailing through another green light at Foothills and Pearl.

"Did Basil and B. J. get along okay?" she asked.

Now Mrs. Underwood did seem startled. "Get along?"

"Yeah. Did they fight about anything?"

Mrs. Underwood pinched her lips together and shook her head.

Foothills and what? Did Walnut intersect?

"Mrs. Underwood, Basil's death is being ruled an accident. Are you satisfied with that?"

The woman squeezed her eyelids shut, and her head changed course to a nod.

"Are you okay here with B. J.? Would you like to talk to somebody from social services? A counselor? Maybe a minister?"

Foothills and Arapahoe.

For precious seconds, Mrs. Underwood stood unmoving, her whole face clenched. Then she batted her eyes open. "What would I want to talk about?"

"Basil's death? Betsy's death? B. J. moving in with you?" Hearing a car motor, Maxey backed toward the front door. "Do you want B. J. living here with you?"

Mrs. Underwood rubbed at her forehead and the cigarette in that hand trailed a graceful contrail. "I'd rather it was Betsy," she whimpered.

Maxey glanced out the door as the car came into view. A blue station wagon full of kids and dogs, it puttered on up the street. She might have another five minutes before B. J. came roaring up, but she didn't want to find out. She scrabbled for a business card in the pocket of her shoulder bag, found one, dropped it on the floor, creased it trying to pick it up, held it out to Mrs. Underwood.

"If you need help, or if you think of anything you'd like to tell me, please call," she said, reaching for the storm door latch.

"It sticks. Kick it at the bottom."

With the full force of Maxey's anxiety behind it, her kick would have given the Denver Broncos an extra point after. She spilled out onto the stoop and trotted to the Toyota. She took a convoluted route back to the office, driving south and west before heading north, all the while watching for black convertibles with, possibly, gun muzzles for hood ornaments.

"What if B. J. killed Basil?" Maxey leaned on the kitchen table, her shoulders hunched to her ears, eating an apple.

Beside her, Calen methodically peeled an orange, the golden skin coiling round and round in one long strip. "Sweetheart, we don't have anything pointing to foul play in Basil Underwood's death. Everything indicates an accident with a cigarette."

"Maybe B. J. killed Betsy, too. Maybe Basil found out,

and that's why B. J. killed him."

Calen sighed hard. "You can 'maybe' all you like. Just don't do it when anyone else but me is around."

"B. J. said he moved in with Mrs. Underwood because she was too confused to live alone, but she didn't seem confused today. She was really enjoying looking through the old photos in the family album. Tell me this. If he's such a devoted nephew, how come there weren't any pictures of him in the album? Huh? Betsy visits him in California and all of a sudden she's dead and he's insinuated himself in the Underwood household. And Aunt Lenora slips up and calls him Betsy sometimes."

Calen finished skinning the orange and broke it apart, releasing a mist of juice. "You think B. J. is Betsy. Is that it?"

"I did until I saw him. He's not the right shape, his face isn't the same, and he's got whiskers. But there's something funny going on, that's for sure. Otherwise, why would B.J. get in such a snit over my talking to Mrs. Underwood about her children?" She twirled the apple core by its stem. "How can I find out exactly what happened to Betsy?"

Calen chewed and swallowed. "County clerk. Vital records. You'd have to fill out a form requesting a death certificate."

Maxey used her napkin to mop at the juice running into his beard. "Here or in California?"

He shrugged.

The refrigerator cycled on, making the watering can on top of it jig and jingle. The kitchen windows had darkened into gray mirrors. Maxey watched her shadowy self take another bite of apple. Calen's shadowy self leaned back and stretched, which Maxey recognized as an unconscious signal he was working up his nerve to do or say something.

"You know, I've been spending a lot of time here," he said.

"Yeah. I like that."

"But my place is bigger. With a nice yard."

"Yeah?"

"Well, I just thought, maybe you'd like to, you know, come over there."

Maxey had to laugh. "I've heard of un-birthdays. This must be an un-marriage proposal."

He laughed too, but his eyes watched her, alert and wary. "Is that what it sounds like?"

"I do come to your house sometimes," she said. "Every Saturday morning you let me do my laundry in your wonderful washer and dryer."

"You're right. Wouldn't you like to eliminate the drive across town?" He popped the last bit of orange into his mouth and started to stand.

Maxey yanked him down again and hooked her knee over his to hold him there. "Wait a minute. You don't get off that easy. Are you suggesting I could move into your house?" She laughed, in case he wasn't suggesting that.

"Why not?"

"Why?"

"Your stairs are too steep and you don't have a garage."

"I couldn't walk to work from Table Mesa."

He rubbed her thigh draped over his. "Is that it? The best argument against it you can think of?"

"Well, I like this place. I've lived here a lot of years."

"I have a patio, a water bed, and the aforementioned washer and dryer."

"I'd hate to leave Ollie Kraig alone in the house. I'd hate to keep paying rent on it when I wasn't using the apartment."

"That last is a pro, not a con. We consolidate and cut our housing costs in half."

"Sure," Maxey said, pinching the tip of his nose, still teasing him to protect herself. "And then if we have a fight, you throw me out and I have to live in my car. You've got to give me a better reason to change my address."

So he did, finally. He said, "I love you," and his kiss said it, too.

"I don't want to get married," Maxey said, when her mouth was free, still too damned unsure of herself and of Calen to lobby for that next, logical step.

He leaned away from her. "Maxey—"

The telephone shrilled. Maxey groaned. Calen didn't loosen his hold, and on the fourth ring, the answering machine switched on.

Beeep.

"Maxey, sweetheart, this is Ollie Kraig downstairs."

Maxey grinned at his thinking he had to identify himself that thoroughly, as if she knew Ollies all over town, all of whom called her "sweetheart."

"I wondered if you could come down and discuss our trick or treat plans for Monday night. I'll be here this evening whenever it's convenient for you to drop in."

Calen finally relaxed his grip, his arms still a circle around her.

"I'll go now," she said over Ollie's slow, tremulous sign-off. "It won't take long. All it is is the two of us are going to hand out treats at Ollie's, so he won't have to keep answering the bell by himself."

"You could shut off all the lights and hide out in the back of the house. Eat the candy yourselves."

"What are you—some kind of Halloween Scrooge?" She gently extracted herself from his embrace. "Is that what you're doing the thirty-first?"

"You kidding? I've got a Darth Vader costume and a goodies bag the size of a pillow case. I'll be ringing your bell at about eight."

"You can ring my bell anytime." Her Mae West impression needed work. She scooted her chair back, tied an errant shoelace, and headed for the door.

"Can't you just call him on the phone?"

"I'll be right back. Save my place." She ran down the stairs.

Emerging on the front porch, she paused to breathe the night air with appreciation. A nippy wind swirled through, showering leaves from their branches and skittering them along the sidewalk. Spruce Street hummed with more activity than usual for this time of evening. None of the immediate neighbors partied much, but tonight someone was trying hard to make up for that. The curbs teemed with parked cars, one of which disgorged a costumed quartet—great hulking shapes who hailed Maxey as she crossed the porch to Ollie's door.

"Is this the way to Vlad the Impaler's?"

"I know the way, Igor. Don't frighten the poor woman."

"Where's the moon? Yip-yip-yee-ouch! Somebody get off my tail."

"Double, double, toil and trouble."

"Triple, triple, gorge and tipple."

The group disappeared up the street, howling with laughter and just plain howling.

Maxey rapped at Ollie's storm door and scrubbed at her chilly arms. The wind swooped through the porch and seemed to whisper her name. She jogged in place, wishing Ollie would hurry up, feeling oddly spooked and ashamed of it.

The overhead porch light lit, crackled, and died. Damn. Now she'd have to get the ladder and replace the burned-out bulb. Ollie's silhouette leaned into the windowed door and the chain lock rattled.

"'Axey," the wind breathed. "'A-a-a-xey."

Maxey yanked open the storm door and nearly bowled Ollie over as she crowded inside.

"Sorry! It's cold out there."

"You should have worn a jacket," Ollie scolded. "Come into the kitchen and have some hot coffee."

When elderly Mrs. Waterford had owned the house and lived in this part of it, the rooms smelled of Ivory soap and peaches, and every piece of furniture showcased Mrs. W.'s talent for housekeeping. During Ollie's residency, the predominant scent was cigar, and the furniture squatted almost invisible under layers of magazines, newspapers and books.

Maxey liked his casual version of home as much as she'd liked Mrs. Waterford's tidy one. A person would never get bored here, surrounded by enough reading material to wallpaper the entire house.

Ollie measured instant coffee into two white mugs and put water on to boil. Maxey lifted a dictionary off a chrome and plastic kitchen chair and sat down.

"The deal is, I make the cookies, you man the door," Ollie said, getting immediately down to business. His skimpy white hair needed a comb, his gray whiskers needed a razor, his blue dress shirt needed a couple of buttons.

"You don't have to make cookies, Ollie. The kids like store-bought candy. I'll pick up several bags at the grocery."

"Oh. Well, how about if I bake cookies for you and me, then?" He rubbed his nose with the back of a spotted hand.

"I'll eat some of the candy, thanks."

"Drat." Ollie ducked his head to peer out the kitchen window at the blackness.

"What's the matter?"

"The garage doors aren't latched. The wind's giving them a good shake."

She'd been hearing the thumps, she realized, ever since she'd come into the kitchen. Ollie reached for an aged leather jacket draped on the back of one chair.

"I'll do it," Maxey said, standing up.

"Wear this, then." Ollie dropped the jacket over her shoulders before she could insist she didn't need it. It smelled of old cow and old man.

She opened the back door, made sure it shut tight behind her, crossed the wooden porch to the grass yard, and hurried toward the detached garage that parked at the edge of the alley.

She circled around to the side, where the twin wooden doors, splintered and full of knotholes, secured Ollie's Plymouth from nothing except rain and snow. There was no lock, not even a padlock anymore, and the space inside was just big enough to hold one mid-sized automobile with no room on either side to get in and out without sucking up one's stomach.

A lamp on a pole several yards down the alley begrudged her enough light to see the dangling hasp and the partially open door that swung back and forth.

Sliding her arms into the sleeves of the jacket, Maxey reached for the farther door. The wind pushed against her face, lifting her hair off her forehead. She turned her back to it, shoved the doors together and fumbled for the pin.

That's when a presence loomed behind her and enveloped her in black. Fighting against the unwanted hug, she drew air for a startled scream.

"Be quiet," a growly voice commanded in her ear. "I will cut your throat if you say one word. I am Jack the Ripper."

He hadn't told her not to struggle. Dreading the knife she expected to rip into her at any second, she braced her legs and thrashed her arms, searching for leverage, for a lucky hit, for mercy.

He struggled just as hard to keep the advantage, his front pressed into her back. "I'll slice you," he panted. "Stick you and rend."

Let this be a stupid joke, a Halloween prankster, so I'll be alive tomorrow to sue his goddamn ass.

"Say your prayers, missy." His whisper spittled her ear. "Say good-bye to the big, beautiful world."

She figured she might as well scream. She didn't think being quiet would save her. That's when she discovered she couldn't produce so much as a squeak. Terror had rendered all systems no-go. Her knees unlocked, her arms lolled, and she hung in Jack's grasp, a dead weight.

Her uselessness dragged him down with her till they were kneeling, his rough overcoat surrounding her like a nightmare. It smelled of mothballs and underarm perspiration. She had never fainted in her life; all the conditions seemed perfect for a good, old-fashioned swoon.

Whap!

The wind threw open the loose garage door, smashing it against Jack's left shoulder. Grunting, he tipped sideways, allowing Maxey to rally her senses and crab-scuttle the other direction. In a wash of fresh adrenaline, she picked up a baseball-sized rock and began thumping Jack, aiming for his head but batting zero, all her swings whiffing off his shoulders.

Fending her off, one arm shielding his face with the greatcoat, Dracula-style, he rolled to his feet and retreated into the shadowed yard. "I'll be back when you least expect me."

His footsteps pounded through the side yard, and then all Maxey could hear was the muttering wind—and her blood, all of it still safely inside, roaring in her head.

She crouched, stunned, afraid to move, afraid not to move, afraid. Her ears ached with the effort to hear any sound of her attacker still lurking in the shadows. After a moment, feeling truly alone, she remembered who she was and why she was here.

She dropped the rock, pushed herself up off the ground, dusted her hands, turned, and latched the garage doors in only four tries. Wrapping Ollie's jacket tight around her, she wobbled her way back to the house. She wasn't dead, but she felt like a zombie.

Ollie didn't glance up from his newspaper, spread beside his coffee mug on the table.

"I got the garage closed up," Maxey said, shrugging off the jacket and returning it to the chair.

"Thanks. Your coffee's getting cold."

She sat down and tossed it back like a cowboy drinking rotgut whiskey. She stood up again. "So I'll see you Monday about six."

"Sounds good." Ollie squinted up at her. "You feel okay? You look a little peaked."

"I'm tired." Her tongue was almost too thick for the words. "See you."

Opening the front door, she cringed back from the dark outside. Taking a breath, she stepped from the golden glow of the living room into the gloom again. The porch floor wheezed underfoot. The party up the street manifested itself in rock music and uninhibited laughter.

Maxey flitted to her door and threw herself inside, into the warm, lighted stairwell. Twisting the deadbolt to lock felt like one huge sigh of relief. She hauled herself upstairs, two at a time, hoping to reach the top and Calen before her control exploded all to hell.

7

"What's the use of calling the police, Calen? The jerk's long gone. They can't do anything."

"Maxey, the police need to know about this. What if he's out there terrorizing some other woman right now?"

"No! It was me he wanted. He called me 'Missy,' but he also called me by name. He was hiding near the house and he taunted me—'A-a-a-xey.'"

"Knowing your name doesn't mean that he won't attack somebody else since he failed with you."

She covered her eyes with one hand, elbow on the table. "God, you're right."

Straightening up from his squat beside her chair, Calen patted Maxey's shoulder as he walked to the telephone.

She spread her hands, palms up on the table and stared dully at the dirt on them. The tips of three fingers on the right one—her rock hand—were split and raw. Till now, she hadn't felt the damage. It sent her scrambling to the bathroom mirror to check her neck, afraid he'd cut her after all and the weight of her head might rip the wound wide open.

Patrolman Emilio Madrid arrived to take Maxey's complaint. He sat on the edge of the couch, memo book on his knee, taking notes. "Describe him for me."

"I can't. It was dark and he came up behind me. He had on this big wool cloak or coat."

She took a swig of the Coke Calen had set in front of her and appreciated having a leakproof throat to carry it to her stomach. She felt rooted in the dinette chair pulled in close to the table; she couldn't imagine ever leaving it to venture out into the world again.

"You think you can't describe him, but you may know more than you realize." Madrid clicked his ballpoint pen in and out. "When he had hold of you, did you get an idea of his height, weight, maybe?"

"Oh. Oh, sure. He was a little taller than me. About five-eight? Not fat but sturdy."

"Did you grab at his hair? Or happen to touch his face?" Madrid dabbed at his own brown moustache.

Reluctantly, Maxey put herself back in Jack's clutches and pictured herself groping his head. "He had a scarf on!" She looked at Calen, who beamed at her for dredging up this puny fact. "Tight on the top of his head, knotted in back, like a pirate or a football player. I don't remember touching his face," she added, disappointed she couldn't add a full beard and an eye patch to her triumph of the scarf.

"How about the voice?"

"He whispered real loud." She shrugged.

"Any impediment or accent?"

"Can a person whisper in an accent?"

"Oh, sure."

"I guess not then."

"And you didn't see the knife?"

"No, not a glimmer of it, and I didn't feel it either." Maxey jutted her jaw. "I bet he didn't even have one."

"When you're in a situation like that, you don't want to gamble that your assailant is lying," Madrid said, and Calen, leaning against the counter between kitchen and living room, nodded solemnly. "Do you have any suspicion who this was that attacked you?"

"Uh." She glanced at Calen, who gave her no sign what to say. "I don't *know*, as in *for a fact*. I didn't recognize him."

"But you have an educated guess," Madrid coached.

Moe wandered into the room, glared at the policeman for being in his favorite spot, and stalked out again.

Maxey examined her abraded fingers. "Well, there's this one person who's fresh in my mind because he happened to threaten me this afternoon. But I don't want to accuse him, because I just don't know."

"Why don't you give me the name and we'll check it out. We'll see where he was this evening without disclosing why we're asking."

"If you're going to give Officer Madrid that name, you ought to give him the name of the other guy you had a fight with today," Calen said.

Maxey squirmed. "I usually get along fine with everyone," she felt obliged to explain. "I was just having a bad day."

Madrid waited, pen poised.

So Maxey told him about her attempt to interview Mrs. Underwood and about B. J.'s chasing her off. She left out her speculations concerning Basil's death and Betsy's death. The bare bones report made B. J. sound like a paranoid recluse. Maxey thought that about summed him up.

"And the other person you quarreled with?"

Maxey rolled her eyes. "He's a poet—according to him. I refused to publish his stuff in the *Regard*, we had words, and he went away mad. Robert Truet, alias Roberto Trueblood. He lives at the Bluebell House, so if environment has anything to do with it, he's probably Jack the Ripper."

"Uh-huh. Anyone else?"

Maxey didn't take the question seriously. She'd already put her money down on B. J.

Still writing, Madrid asked, "Do you think there's a connection between this incident and the one you called us on last night?"

"I can't imagine what it would be. Can you?" She looked back and forth from man to man.

"Harassment, perhaps?" Calen said. "Someone wanting to get back at you for something you said in the *Regard*?"

She clutched the top of her head. "Why not a simple, lawful, irate letter to the editor? Sheesh."

"Would you publish an irate letter?" Madrid asked.

Maxey's laugh burst out an octave too high. "As long as it wasn't in verse."

Pocketing his notes and promising to be in touch, Madrid left them. For a few minutes, his high-powered search light illuminated the back yard as he prowled it looking for clues.

Ollie telephoned Maxey to ask if she knew what was going on out there, and she had to apologize for not burdening him earlier with her horrible experience. Of course, he blamed himself for letting her go out in the dark by herself, which was why, she realized, she hadn't told him about the attack. It took five minutes of intensive reassurance to give him a bare minimum relief of guilt. Even then, he might have continued apologizing, but Officer Madrid knocked at his door, and Ollie hastened to be interviewed, no doubt confessing responsibility for all but the actual cloak and dagger.

"I was wearing his jacket," Maxey said to Calen after she'd hung up the phone. "If this were a mystery novel, the assailant would have mistaken me for Ollie, and it's really Ollie who's in danger."

"Right. And Jack would have called Ollie 'Missy'."

"Sure he would, after he discovered what nice boobs Ollie had." Maxey's laugh was normal again.

"Well, you're right about one thing—uh, two things."

"I'm starved. Are you hungry?" She rushed to the refrigerator and began unloading it onto the adjoining counter. "Have a Dagwood sandwich with me?"

"Okay."

He came up behind and hugged her, and the affectionate gesture dispelled the afterimage of Jack's embrace. She came within an eyelash of finally crying. But swallowing again and again, she forced herself to listen to what else Calen was saying.

"Perfect timing, huh? Just when you're thinking of getting away from this bad neighborhood? Actually I hired the cretin to stampede you into saying, yes, you'd come live with me."

Maxey twisted open an unlabeled jar and sniffed it, trying to decide if it was leftover gravy or vanilla pudding. "That's exactly why I can't move over to your house now."

Calen stiffened. "I'm kidding. I never met the man."

"No, I mean I can't leave here now. It would look like I'm running away. Scared."

"*Aren't* you scared?"

"Yes."

Calen sighed hard against her neck, making her shiver. "Ms. Burnell, you can be the most exasperating woman."

"Write a letter to the editor," she said, putting away the gravy pudding for another day.

The next morning, Maxey thumped a heaping clothes basket onto the stone slab porch by Calen's front door and hunted his key out of her jeans pocket. Apparently the neighborhood kids were celebrating Saturday by watching cartoons or sleeping late. The narrow, curving street lay quiet and serene.

She hadn't slept well last night, and she blamed that for the dull depression that weighed her down like a black cloak. She'd even snapped at Calen when he asked her if she'd be okay at his house by herself. He needed to finish up some work at the office, but he could come with her and do it Sunday instead, he said. And he'd offered with such tender seriousness, as if she'd just been diagnosed with terminal cold feet. So she blew up at him—not much—enough to add regret to her general stew of unhappiness.

The lock finally acknowledged the twisted key. Holding the door ajar with a knee, Maxey hefted the basket and blundered inside. On the right, Calen's blue and beige living room dozed with all the shades pulled, inviting her to come in and put her feet up. Turning left instead, Maxey wrestled the door open into the car-less garage, where the washer and dryer squatted discreetly behind a bamboo screen.

She loaded in her laundry, and while the tub hissed itself full of hot water, she explored the house, imagining herself living there: the living room, kitchen, bathroom; the study upstairs, the bathroom upstairs, the master bedroom with its cool white walls, white bedspread, white carpet. All of it neat and tidy. Well, of course it was neat and tidy; Calen had been spending all his time at her apartment.

But Calen was a neat and tidy man. His home would look like this even if he were in residence.

Maxey walked to the bedroom window overlooking the green, shade-dappled backyard. As she leaned against the sill, a blur of motion disappeared around the north corner of the house. Lots of deer wandered through these residential areas so close to the foothills. The wildlife merited a check mark in the plus column of her list of reasons for or against moving in with Calen. The first night she had ever spent here with him, she'd sat bolt upright, torn from a sound sleep by a stampede of raccoons clambering and growling across the roof. Maybe the wildlife should be just half a check mark in the plus column.

The distant washing machine chugged tirelessly. Maxey went downstairs to the sun-soaked oak and chrome kitchen. A school of dust motes floating in the light scattered when she slid open the glass patio door.

Someone before Calen had landscaped the little yard into a series of terraces and rock gardens that sloped down to a public pathway boundary. Trees and bushes, no two the same species, zigzagged beside the stepping stone stairs to the bottom. Pillows of chrysanthemums, gold and orange and wine, were strewn around the random patches of grass. A swath of ankle-high copper lamps, a birdbath, a sundial, a fat clay frog—it seemed the ideal environment for once-upon-a-times. Maxey awarded it a double plus on her list.

At the bottom of the yard, a flimsy wire fence marked the end of Calen's territory. His tool shed was tucked into the hillside beside the sorry remains of a vegetable garden too dry for anything but weeds to thrive. Maxey spotted one perfect red tomato to pluck, rub against her jeans, and eat, leaning far over to let the juice and seeds drip.

She returned up the slope, hands in rear pockets, taking long, slow steps, watching out for deer scat. The sun on her hair felt like warm butter. A dove, high and out of sight, mourned. Maxey realized she felt pretty damn good now.

If Calen's place could do that for her, maybe she should take him up on his offer. The thing that worried her was—what if he grew tired of her and wanted her to leave? How could either of them live that down, both the rejecting and the being rejected?

Crossing the brick patio, she slid open the kitchen door and headed for the refrigerator to check out the drink menu. Hand on handle, she paused to listen to something that wasn't quite right.

Instead of the bump and slosh of the washing machine, she heard buttons and zippers hitting the sides of the dryer.

"Calen?"

Not listening for his answer, she opened the refrigerator and took out two cans of Coke. Popping the tab on one, she carried the other into the living room. "Calen?"

By her watch, her clothes should be just beginning the rinse cycle. Calen must have had something in the dryer and turned it on while she was outside.

She strolled up the stairs, expecting him to be in the bathroom with the door shut. Not there. In the garage, then, unable to hear for the pummeling dryer. Sipping at the Coke, she crossed the study to the window to check for his station wagon in the driveway. It wasn't there, and he couldn't have put it in the garage, because her Toyota sat in the way. Had he had car trouble and walked home?

Depositing both cans on the desk blotter, she glided down

the carpeted steps and peeped into the kitchen again before turning toward the garage door. It was closed, and she stalled for a few seconds, a little spooked, trying to recall if she had shut it. Winding the knob around, she gently pushed.

The noise of the dryer escalated. She leaned over the threshold to look. The garage lay deserted. Crossing the no-man's land of empty concrete, Maxey glanced behind the folded screen before moving closer to look into the silent, open-lidded washer—the soapy water appeared empty of clothes. Rubbing at the goosebumps that suddenly prickled her arms, Maxey studied the dial on the dryer. It had forty minutes to go on regular heat. The too-wet laundry inside bumped hard against the metal sides.

"Calen?" she called, her heart not in it. He would never have moved her unfinished washing into the dryer. She stood rooted, staring at the trail of water spots on the floor, trying to be angry at someone's practical joke, but feeling only an escalating apprehension.

Her next step should be to open the dryer door to see if it was really her clothes dancing around in there. She grasped the knob, trying not to picture what else it might be—a body, for instance—and yanked.

The dryer stopped and a wad of tangled bras and T-shirts rolled over and stopped, too. Maxey scraped the basket under the open door and pulled the sopping mess into it, using just her fingertips, wary of foreign objects hidden in the folds—bloody towels or headless snakes or excrement.

When her benign, clean-smelling washing heaped the basket, she remembered to look over her shoulder. She was still alone.

Calen's camping gear was stowed in a wooden chest in the corner beside the little door to the backyard. She walked over to test that locked door. Through the dusty window, the mourning dove sounded closer, more mournful. Maxey unlatched the lid of the chest and lifted out his backpack and sleeping bag to find the red-handled hatchet at the bottom.

Holding it at arm's length straight down, careful to keep

the blade pointed away from her leg, she considered what to do next. She could simply slide up the big double door, walk to her car a few feet outside, drive to the nearest public phone, and call Calen.

But it would be quicker and easier to phone from here, from this house. She could almost swear she was the only occupant at the moment.

Of course, she'd have sworn the same thing half an hour ago, when the laundry fairy was busy spoiling her peaceful morning.

She didn't think the 911 operator would appreciate a complaint about a washing in progress.

The nearest phone hung in the pass-through between living room and kitchen. Circling around to the kitchen side, gliding the glass door open and ready for an emergency evacuation, Maxey lifted the receiver, wondering if there would be a dial tone.

There was. She dialed Calen's office.

"This is Calen Taylor. I'm away from my desk at the moment, but if you leave a message . . . ."

Maxey depressed the button and dialed a different number.

"Boulder Fire Department, Braverman speaking."

She cupped her hand around the mouthpiece and kept her voice low. "This is Maxey Burnell. Could you ring Calen Taylor for me?"

"Ah, I could, but it wouldn't do any good. I saw him leave with Captain Akers a few minutes ago."

She grimaced. "You think he'll be gone long?"

"He didn't say. Can I take a message?"

"Tell him to call home the minute he gets in."

"If it's an emergency, I can try his pager. He might be wearing it."

"Um, no, that's okay. Just tell him whenever he gets back."

She disconnected and dialed again. Twirling the hatchet handle in slow half-circles, she listened to the ringing on the line and the silence of the house.

Scotty aimed the Bronco into the left turning lane at Arapahoe and Twenty-Eighth and eased on the brake. In the back, a plastic sack of groceries slithered and spilled. He'd been to the car wash and to Safeway, and now he was minutes from being home in his house trailer—excuse it, *mobile home*—in the park on Thirtieth Street. He had the day all planned. Two college football games, two rented videos, and at least one nap should about shoot it.

The cellular phone chirped.

He picked it up without looking, feeling comfortable, finally, with the dexterity required to drive, work a telephone, and chew gum at the same time.

"Hi, Maxey," he answered, since she was the only one who ever called him on it.

"Scotty, I hate to bother you."

She'd bothered him already—her voice came through kind of thin and shrill, so he wouldn't have known it was her if he didn't know it was her.

"What's the matter, kiddo?"

"I'm not sure. I'm at Calen's, and I'm supposed to be alone, but someone's here or been here, but I don't want to call the police because the way I know someone's been here is such a damnfool thing."

By now, Scotty had turned left and was trying to think of the quickest way to get pointed back south again. "I'll be there in a minute, but you ought to call the cops, too."

"You remember how to get to Calen's?"

"Refresh my memory." He muscled the Bronco right, into the Crossroads Mall parking lot and headed south to catch the Arapahoe exit, concentrating on Maxey's directions.

"Lock yourself in your car. Lay on the horn if anyone looks cross-eyed at you," he said before breaking the connection and driving in earnest.

***

By the time Calen came home at about one o'clock, Maxey had relaxed enough to doze on the couch beside Scotty, who had taken off his shoes to prop his feet on the coffee table while he watched Colorado buff Oklahoma on Calen's TV.

Straightening up and stretching, Maxey smiled. "Welcome."

The men exchanged nods and remarks about the score before Calen went into the kitchen to break out refreshments. He paused on the way back, having noticed the hatchet lying on the pass-through. He raised his eyebrows but didn't ask.

"You didn't get my message," Maxey said. "To phone home. I bet the guys get tired of taking calls like that."

"I didn't go back to the office after lunch with Cap Akers." He ruffled her hair and then stood back to sip his pop and watch the game. "What did you want?"

Having hashed over the whole thing with Scotty already, she wasn't as enthusiastic in the telling this go-around. By the time she got to the part about the intruder not knowing enough to put a static softener sheet in with the clothes, she had Calen's full attention.

"So then when I couldn't reach you, I reached out and touched Scotty. And he came over and turned on the TV and that's about it."

"You didn't phone the police?"

"No, and you can't make me feel guilty about it. The perpetrator isn't going to be drying some other woman's wash just because he failed to dry mine."

"You're sure nothing is missing?"

"You'd better check around the house, but I know my laundry is all there. I counted the panties and didn't see anything—you know—wrong. Then I threw everything into the washer again."

"Did you count the socks?" Scotty asked, and Maxey grinned with him, remembering a temporary partner at the *Regard*, long gone now, who overzealously admired any well-made shoe on any well-shaped foot, and had also appreciated hosiery, bedroom slippers, and the occasional sock.

Calen went to examine the scene of the crime. Before following him, Maxey watched Jonathan Pryce suave his way through another Infinity commercial. He had her sold, if she ever got a big enough income tax refund.

Patting Scotty's knee, she bounced off the couch and went to the garage. The innocent-looking laundry, folded and stacked high in its yellow plastic basket, occupied the top of the dryer. Calen had squatted to inspect the drum.

Tracing his ear with a finger, Maxey waited for him to find something she'd missed. That was his job, after all.

He stood and put an arm around her. "He followed you here."

"If it's the same Jack."

"It has to be. Two people after you at once? Not unless you ticked off the mafia."

"Somehow I can't picture a godfather issuing an order to dry Maxey Burnell's laundry."

"It's one guy. He's stalking you."

Pretending not to feel the chill that sledded down her spine, she turned under his arm to plant a kiss on his bristly cheek. "Don't worry. I'm going to nail him before he nails me."

"Yeah? How are you going to do that?"

"First thing Monday, I'm going to start tracking Betsy—make sure she really did die accidentally in California. I'm going to spend the day at the courthouse exercising my freedom of information rights, going through tax records, trial records, *stuff*, till I find a lead to what Basil was doing the last ten years. Betsy and B.J., too."

"Sounds like a time consumer."

"Maybe Sylvia, too. Remember Sylvia? Dang. Breaking and entering to steal a couple of cigar boxes doesn't seem like that big a deal anymore."

"You planning to put out a *Regard* this week, are you?"

"I'll get a head start on that by working tomorrow."

"You must be desperate, all right. Working on Sunday."

She grinned as she admitted the obvious. "Then the rest of the week, I'll push most of the work load off on Scotty."

Calen gave her a quick, dismissive squeeze. "I'm going next door to see if the neighbors saw anyone over here."

"Good. I'll come with you. Try the folks on the north first, because I thought someone or something ran around that side of the house when I was admiring the view out the bedroom window."

But the folks on the north weren't home, and from the little pile of newspapers on the door mat, it appeared they hadn't been home earlier either.

Disappointed, Maxey linked elbows with Calen and matched his stride up the sloped street, past his house, to the next one. This looked more promising. A young man and woman wearing white shorts, black sweatshirts and bright green work gloves were twisting a six-foot aspen tree into a freshly dug hole by the front porch. The ball of root thudded into place, and the woman held the trunk straight while the man sifted dirt around it with a shiny shovel that still bore its yellow price label.

Maxey and Calen watched till the tree could stand on its own and the planters stepped back to admire it.

"Looks good, Barry," Calen said, pulling Maxey with him up the driveway.

"I can hardly wait for it to start bearing apples," Barry said, straight-faced.

"Evergreens don't bear fruit," his helpmate sneered.

Maxey laughed while Calen explained that Barry's field was physics and Tracey's was mechanical engineering and this was probably their annual Be Outside Day. They both took off their gloves to shake hands with Maxey,

Calen got to the point. "Did either of you happen to notice anyone skulking around my place in the middle of the day? Besides Maxey, I mean."

"Oh, gosh, no!" Tracey put her hands to her cheeks, her eyes wide and sympathetic before she even heard the problem.

"Somebody broke in the house?" Barry asked.

"Apparently."

"Steal anything?"

"Maxey's peace of mind." Calen cleared his throat and scuffed a sneaker toe at sand on the driveway.

Maxey smiled to herself, recognizing his embarrassment. Now maybe he could understand why she hadn't called the police.

"How about a black convertible?" she asked. "A Ford, I think—older model with a bad top. Did you see a car like that parked or cruising around here today?"

The McCutcheons shook their heads. A motor ground into life up the street and all four heads turned to watch what came by. It was a red pick-up, and the kid driving looked young enough to need a booster seat.

Refusing Barry's offer of a beer and accepting Tracey's invitation to "come over for barbecue sometime," Maxey and Calen headed across the street toward a porch guarded by fierce-faced pumpkins.

The young couple there hadn't seen a stranger or the convertible either. They suggested Maxey and Calen come over for a barbecue some evening.

The rest of the neighborhood survey failed to locate anyone who'd noticed anything unusual. There were two more offers of barbecue.

Calen draped an arm over Maxey's shoulders as they trudged homeward, uphill on the curve of street. Clouds had crowded in over the foothills like a white log jam. The afternoon darkened and turned chilly.

"No children on this street?" Maxey asked.

"Hum. No, no little ones. Most everyone's associated with the university, career-oriented."

"You ought to have a block party, get all those dinner parties over at once."

"Good idea. You can organize it."

"Forget I mentioned it."

Tree leaves rustled. An automatic sprinkler spat and came full on. The air smelled of charcoal lighter fluid.

Maxey gave Calen's neighborhood a check mark on the pro side of her list to-move-or-not-to-move.

Back at Calen's house again, she did call the police station to ask Emilio Madrid whether B. J. or Robert had alibis for the previous night. Supposedly B. J. had been helping his aunt can pumpkin, and Robert was reading chapters three through five of *War and Peace*. Maxey could just bet they were engaged in equally sterling activities this morning while she was being terrorized by Mr. Clean.

8

Maxey loved evenings like this, when the air's chilly bite cleared her head and energized her limbs. She'd talked Calen into coming downtown to try a freshly opened buffet restaurant. All that talk of barbecues had made her ravenous. Squeezing Calen's elbow to her chest, she hustled him along the Pearl Street promenade, dodging fellow rosy-cheeked pedestrians and an occasional gorilla, vampire, or other anomaly of the season.

"Won't this place be packed?" Calen raised his voice above the mournful wheeze of an accordion played by a young woman dressed as Snow White. "New restaurants always are. Plus, they usually aren't up to speed on their service for the first week or two."

"Right. We're in no real hurry, are we? If you don't count being starved?"

"I thought you needed to start the next issue of the *Regard*."

"Whoa," Maxey said, stopping dead.

"You forgot?"

"No, look. A street artist."

She tugged Calen toward the grass median, where a burly man sat on a director's chair, sweeping a fat pencil over the sketchpad on his knees. He glanced up and down, his eyes as busy as his hand, while his model, a solemn little girl, sat unblinking and rigid, as if her least movement would blur the results.

He'd staked out his territory with a dozen caricatures leaning on brass easels. Maxey sidled closer to inspect them. Grinning, she motioned Calen over.

"Look. Here's Morrie."

Calen looked and grinned too.

"Isn't it amazing how a cartoon can look so much like the real person?" Maxey marveled, slowly circling around the rest of the display.

"Let's have him do you," Calen suggested, strolling in her wake.

"I don't think I want my faults exaggerated. Oh!"

"What?"

"It's Sylvia." Maxey squatted down to study the portrait.

The artist had emphasized her shaggy dark hair and eyebrows, the turned-down slice of mouth. Below the impossibly thin neck, her fringed jacket was suggested by no more than five, sure lines.

Maxey lifted it off the easel and held it gingerly, showing the back to Calen. "Is there a price?"

"Five dollars," the artist said without turning his head. "Ten dollars if I do you or your friend. But five for that one."

Maxey rooted into her shoulder bag. Calen drew out his wallet, pinched out a five-dollar bill, and offered it to the artist before she'd excavated past her sunglasses and a wad of Kleenex. The man stuffed it into his shirt pocket, still not looking up from his work.

Maxey peeked over his shoulder as he finished with a flourished signature. He'd played up his model's eyes and straight bangs, de-emphasizing her mouth and chin. When he showed the picture to the girl, she sagged with relief and giggled, displaying braces. Her parents, who'd been waiting on a near-by bench, arrived to admire, pay, and move on.

"Ask you something?" Maxey addressed the artist.

He finally looked at her. His brilliant blue eyes sparkled below the bushy overhang of his eyebrows, and his pink mouth smiled in its nest of reddish moustache and beard. "Ask. I'm best at multiple choice questions."

"Have you ever drawn a face the way police artists do? You know, from a witness's description? Could you do that?"

He shrugged. "Sure. Haven't, but could, if the witness is good at remembering and verbalizing. It wouldn't be a caricature, though."

"No, that's fine. A more realistic sketch is what I'd want." She glanced at Calen who had been edging away. He folded his arms and waited.

"It would take a little longer. I'd have to charge you more," the artist said. "Twenty, twenty-five bucks."

"Okay."

"Did you want to try it now?"

"No, you've got other customers." She smiled at a family—mom, dad, and twin toddlers as busy as corn popping—who waited a few yards away. "What time do you quit here?"

"Usually about nine."

"Would you meet me at the *Regard* newspaper office at about nine-fifteen? That's in the next block—" She pointed.

"I know where it is. Zeb Crespo." He offered his hand.

She shifted Sylvia's picture to her left to clasp his meaty palm. "Maxey Burnell. See you after nine."

Taking exaggerated giant steps to show Calen she was hurrying, she grabbed his arm and shepherded him toward their original destination.

"Who do you want him to draw? Whom."

"I want B. J.'s likeness to show around. To Derrick Sikes and some other people. And I'm chicken to hide in the neighbors' hedge with a telephoto lens and get it myself."

"Thank God for that," Calen said, and then moaned at glimpsing the line of customers outside the new restaurant. "'The Hungry U,' indeed."

"The forehead's too wide," Maxey said. "Up and down.

A lower hairline, I mean."

Zeb sat in her office chair, his left ankle resting on his right knee, the sketch pad propped on the L of his leg. Maxey perched on the office table behind him, watching over his shoulder as he followed her directions for constructing B. J.'s face. Calen wandered around the room, probably toting up fire code violations, now and then pausing to check the artistic work in progress.

So far they had the shape of a face, the hair, eyebrows, the suggestion of eyes, a definite nose. Zeb drew the hairline a fraction closer to the eyebrows. He blocked off the lower face with his wide hand. "Does that look better?"

"Yes."

"Let's concentrate on the mouth for a minute. Lips thin or full?"

"Full. And mean."

He laughed. "Sorry, I don't know how to draw mean."

"Sure you do." She leaned down to point. "Put a fang sticking out, here and here."

Ignoring her, he penciled an unsmiling mouth. "Bigger or smaller than this?"

She thought about it. "Smaller."

He wielded a blob of kneaded eraser, sketched again. "How about the philtrum? Pronounced or not?"

Now Maxey laughed. "I guess not. Surely I'd remember a pronounced philtrum."

"The vertical depression that runs from your nose to your upper lip," Zeb enlightened her.

"Oh, *that* philtrum." She wracked her brain for a second or two. "I don't remember."

"We won't pronounce it then. How about the distance between nose and mouth. Look about right?"

Calen toured close enough to peer at the picture and squeeze Maxey's knee.

After about ten circuits of the room and knee squeezes later, he examined the finished portrait. "Not a bad-looking guy."

"I *told* you we needed fangs," Maxey said to Zeb. She held the picture at arm's length and squinted one-eyed at it. "Astounding. How you could draw someone you haven't seen, just from someone else's description. This is B. J. Underwood, all right."

Whoever B. J. Underwood was.

Maxey spent Sunday morning at the *Regard* office, mostly laboring on advertising layouts. She walked to her apartment at noon to feed Moe and herself, and, feeling self-righteous, returned to work at the office. She liked the conditions—door locked, phone quiet. She accomplished twice as much as if it were a regular day with a regular day's interruptions.

There was one interruption. The children's parade streamed past in mid-afternoon. Maxey gave herself a coffee break and stood with her cup at the front door, enjoying the costumes, the music—courtesy of a tambourine and comb marching band—and the joyful energy emanating from the swarm of little bodies. Their adult chaperones ambled along the fringes like cowboys driving precious livestock.

Maxey remembered Halloweens in her own kidhood, her homemade costumes, beginning with a sweet, pink fairy and getting less glamourous and more gross every year. Her last trick-or-treat night, when she felt obliged to stoop, in order to look young enough, she was an abominable snowwoman.

The parade skipped and bounded up the street, and Maxey turned back to her work, grateful that the only cloaks or pirate scarves she'd seen had been size extra-extra-small.

Monday. October 31. Maxey chewed at a slice of buttered toast, glumly regarding the calendar magnetized to her refrigerator. November arrived tomorrow. "'Winter is icummen in,'" she said, quoting Scotty quoting Ezra Pound. "'Lhude sing Goddamm.'"

What was she so depressed about? She had a good start

on this week's paper. She had her health, a trace of money in the bank, a roof over her head. The promise of another roof over her head.

She'd slept alone last night, without seeing or hearing from Calen at all on Sunday. They'd had another little argument Saturday night. He thought she needed him following her around, watching her back for her. She said she'd simply get some protective Mace spray. He asked how she could compare him to a can of gas. She made the mistake of joking that the mace would never leave up the toilet seat. The discussion was all downhill from there. Still, she thought they had kissed and made up. She had, anyway.

Maybe he was trying the old absence-makes-the-heart-really-appreciate-you route, to stampede her into renting a U-Haul and moving across town, lock, stock, and tomcat.

Judging by her present mood, Calen's strategy might be working.

Carrying the two drawings face to face with a piece of paper toweling between, Maxey let herself into Hill's Office Supply. Derrick wasn't yet open for business next door.

"Help you?" Mrs. Hill sang out from the back of the room. "Oh, hello," she added with a little less enthusiasm when she saw who had come in.

"I'm looking for a big folder," Maxey said, to reassure Mrs. Hill that she was a customer today.

"How big?"

Maxey held up the drawings.

Mrs. Hill frowned. "I won't have a folder that size. How about an art portfolio?"

"Is it expensive?"

Mrs. Hill had turned to walk toward the rear of the store. She half-turned back. "About ten dollars."

"Whoops. Too much."

Rubbing her forehead with the flat of one hand, Mrs. Hill thought for a couple of seconds. "I can give you ten per cent off, but that's still going to be about nine dollars and tax."

"I'll just look around for a minute. Maybe I'll see something I can make do. You have a photocopy machine, don't you?"

"Four of them. Under the balcony, back there."

Mrs. Hill hadn't smiled yet. Her eyes had the dull, glazed look that usually signified a headache. Maybe she, too, had noticed that tomorrow was November.

Maxey followed her past gondolas of tape, envelopes, labels, and enough plastic ware to over-organize every desktop within a half mile radius.

Mrs. Hill arrived at the quartet of humming copy machines lined up under the mezzanine. "Do you need help getting started?"

"Please. Can any of your machines reproduce something this large?" Maxey spread the two portraits apart, face up, on the lid of the nearest copier.

"Uhh," Mrs. Hill exhaled, as if a pain had come and gone. Her eyes twitched back and forth between Sylvia's and B. J.'s faces.

Intrigued by this reaction, Maxey tapped B. J.'s chin. "I know you knew Sylvia. Do you know him?"

"No. How do you know I knew Sylvia?"

"Everyone in downtown Boulder knew Sylvia."

"What do you have these pictures for?"

There was truculence in the woman's voice. Maxey tried not to stare at Mrs. Hill while studying Mrs. Hill. Her gray hair bushed out around her colorless face. Her dull eyes had sharpened, and her mouth pouted in a thoughtful, disapproving cant. She looked a bit like Moe pondering revenge after a trip to the vet's.

"I'm trying to find out more about both these people," Maxey said. "This is B. J. Underwood, Basil Underwood's cousin. Are you certain you never saw him around here?"

"Positive." Mrs. Hill didn't recheck the picture. "You think he had something to do with that poor boy's death?"

"No," Maxey said, mindful of libel. "I'm just curious."

"Here. This machine will do eleven by seventeen. It'll cut off a little on the sides, maybe. You put the original face down in the middle. How many copies you want?" Mrs. Hill's hand trembled as she picked up the drawing of B. J. to demonstrate.

"Just a couple of each. I can always come back if I need more."

The copier sucked and thumped and spat. A clean black and white duplicate of B. J.'s face oozed into the exit tray.

The front door banged, and Mrs. Hill twisted from the hips to check who had come in. Maxey recognized Mr. Hill by his gray aura and his deliberate pace. He carried a white bakery bag, which obviously represented one of the more pleasant parts of the Hills' long-established daily routine.

He plodded along the center aisle and would have continued past them to the back of the building, but Maxey snatched one of the copies of B. J. out of the tray and called to him.

"Mr. Hill, have you seen this man? Especially have you seen him around the store here?"

He veered toward her, his face as stoic as a zombie's and with not much better color. He stopped two yards away to examine the picture Maxey held in front of herself. His expression didn't change.

"No." He cleared his throat. "No." He looked past Maxey at his wife for an unblinking moment, turned, and finished his trek to the office.

Mrs. Hill, apparently assuming Maxey had received enough training, left her to copy Sylvia on her own. Maxey finished and gathered up all the sheets of faces. Mrs. Hill waited at the cash register, keeping busy with a pricing gun that she stamped through a stack of invoice books as if she were killing bugs.

"I guess this is all I need today," Maxey said.

"Forty-three cents. You want a bag?"

"Please." She felt guilty taking a brown bag that probably wiped out the profit from her puny purchase, but that same brown bag could substitute nicely for a ten-buck artist portfolio.

"Are you going to write about Sylvia in the paper again? And this initials guy?"

"Maybe. Sylvia, for sure. Do you have any anecdotes about her I might use? Did she come in here often?"

Mrs. Hill picked up the pricing gun and resumed whacking the merchandise. "A nuisance, she was. You can put that in the paper—'informed sources say she was a nuisance.'"

"In what way?"

"Every way. Wandering around the store, fingering everything, never buying anything. She never stole anything that I know of, but she looked like she would, so we'd have to stop what we were doing so we could keep an eye on her." Mrs. Hill squared up the stack of invoice books with two smart raps on the counter. "Oh, well. She's history now."

Mrs. Hill probably didn't realize the aptness her epithet. Sylvia would go down in Boulder's archives as the eccentric Packy, a town character, whose pedestrian behaviors might gradually be exaggerated into legend. Every truth that Maxey could uncover would be stored on microfilm at the public library for future browsers of old newspapers. She'd never considered that responsibility before. Considering it now made Maxey stand a little straighter.

She folded down the top of her big paper bag, ready to leave. "You may have kept a sharp eye on Sylvia, but I'll bet she was invisible to a lot of the mall merchants. I mean, she cruised in and out of stores all the time, never buying anything, not bothering anything. Harmless. So people would tend to ignore her. Don't you think?"

"Well. Possibly. What's your point?"

"I'm not sure."

Actually, Maxey was sure, but not willing to voice her suspicion. Maybe Sylvia had seen something somewhere that someone hadn't wanted her to see. Maybe someone thought she had picked up something somewhere they didn't want her to have. That would explain the theft of the two junk boxes from Maxey's bookcase.

Would it also explain Sylvia's falling down the Bluebell's flight of stairs?

Boom, boom, boom, kaboom, boom. Derrick's stereo proclaimed the Futon Lode open for business.

Maxey tried to believe that the futon store smelled better today, but her nose wouldn't let her. She walked the length of the deserted showroom, peeped into the unoccupied office, and negotiated the swinging half-doors into the still empty, still blackened receiving area. The back door stood open, so she kept on going, outside, where Derrick and a push broom were tidying up the alley around a rusty-brown dumpster.

Seeing Maxey, he leaned on the broom and flashed his usual happy-go-hopeful smile. "What's up?"

"I brought a picture of Cousin B. J. Underwood for you to peruse." She rustled the original sketch out of her brown bag and held it high at arm's length, where they both could study it.

Derrick considered, stroking his chin. He set the broom against the wall of the building and took the sketch in both hands, staring down at it. Maxey felt a niggle of excitement at his obvious interest.

"Nope," he said. "Stranger to me."

"Oh. Darn."

"But there's something about his eyes—"

Maxey stepped closer to reach past Derrick's arm and block off the lower half of B. J.'s face with her open hand. Derrick, dressed all in shiny black today, smelled like coffee.

"Yeah," he said. "I guess what it is—he resembles Betsy and Basil. Got all their features, only a little skewed, you know?"

"But he isn't them? I mean, this face couldn't be Betsy or Basil, in disguise, say?"

"Aww, no!" Laughing, Derrick handed over the sketch. "Basil's dead. And so's Betsy, you said."

"Yes, but what if I was wrong? Could this be Betsy?"

Derrick took another prolonged look. "You think this is Betsy? No way. This guy's heavier-featured. He's got whiskers, right?"

"Uh-huh."

"Well there you go. Anybody could get a fake beard, but how could a person do fake whiskers?"

"If they can put a man on the moon. . . ." Maxey shrugged.

"Naw. This is a cousin, like he told you. I'd bet my business on it." Derrick grinned to show he recognized what a sucker bet that would be.

Maxey's next stop was the Urban Cowboy. A narrow hall of a store with the merchandise shelved to the ceiling and hung from the rafters, it sold everything a survivalist might need, from Chapstick to camouflage boxer shorts. Maxey walked past the pith helmets, first aid kits, and folding shovels to a rack with signage that screamed in red letters, *PERSONAL PROTECTION DEFENSIVE SPRAYS!* She studied the various sizes of canisters until a guy in a black dress shirt, black pants, black combat boots, and a desert camouflage necktie asked if he could help her.

"This stuff is better than Mace?"

"No comparison. This is red hot cayenne pepper spray. Works on the body's mucous membranes. Instantly. Blinds temporarily. Paralyzes everything but life-support breathing. Mace is tear gas. Takes three to ten seconds to work. Doesn't faze the guy if he's psychotic, drunk, on drugs. Mace's got a shelf life of two years. Pepper spray lasts forever."

"Oh." Maxey couldn't believe she was standing here trying to decide how best to wipe out someone. She picked out the forty-two-ounce pocket/purse size—*fifteen one second blasts*—and handed it to the clerk.

"This's got a non-inflammatory propellant," he said, ringing up nine-ninety-five plus tax. "No risk of fire if he's smoking a cigarette."

"Wonderful." She accepted the can back and stuck it into her fleece jacket pocket, patting the outside to show that it fit.

"Have a nice day," he said without apparent irony.

Maxey spent much of the rest of that day, phone to her ear, grimacing and sighing a lot. Hampered by not knowing exactly where or when Betsy Underwood had allegedly been killed in a California car wreck, Maxey wasted ten per cent of her time trying to get the phone numbers of agencies that might help her, ten per cent being told she had the wrong department, and what seemed like one hundred per cent listening to recorded messages list menus: If you want to speak to a human being who will disconnect you while trying to transfer your call, press . . . .

Scotty stayed out of her way, worked diligently on Thursday's stories, brought her noon refreshment from the Deli, and spoke only when spoken to. He'd have seemed too good to be true except he kept humming golden oldies while he worked. Maxey considered it a small price to pay, especially since Scotty stayed on key, most of the time.

While she ate the pastrami sandwich and sipped the iced tea that Scotty had presented her, she thought of Calen. He hadn't called again today. Was he really mad at her? Good God, maybe he'd fallen in the shower and been lying unconscious for two days!

Grabbing up the phone, still chewing, she punched in his office number.

"Taylor." He sounded mad and he didn't even know yet it was she who was calling.

"Hi, Calen." She tried to say it in her sexiest voice, the effect spoiled considerably by a mouthful of bread.

"Hi, Maxey. What's wrong?"

"What do you mean what's wrong?" She swallowed

hard and took a hasty swig of tea.

"You don't usually call me in the middle of the day."

"No, well—surprise!"

"So what do you need?"

"What do you mean what do I need?" Her voice sharpened.

"Come on, Maxey, don't take everything I say wrong. I just meant that all the bad stuff that's been happening to you lately makes me expect to get calls in the middle of a work day announcing some new problem."

"*Announcing* a new problem? Announcing? You think I'm grandstanding—looking for sympathy? Enjoying the drama?"

Scotty quietly exited his chair and hustled to shut himself in the restroom.

"Bad word choice. I didn't mean—" Calen was saying when she interrupted him.

"Calen, I just called to see if *you* were okay. Obviously you are. I'll talk to you again some time better for both of us."

"Okay. Maybe tonight. You want me to pick you up at the office?"

She opened her mouth to say, yes, let's have dinner somewhere semi-expensive.

But Calen kept talking, and his next words made her pinch her lips shut. "You're walking, right? Wait for me. I might be as late as seven, but I don't want you walking home that late alone, so wait for me."

"You know I can't do that. I'm supposed to help Ollie with trick-or-treaters before seven."

"Maxey—"

"Don't worry. I've got my trusty pepper spray. I'll be at the house whenever you can get away from all that work."

"Fine. Don't wait up."

"Fine." She hurried to hang up the phone before he could hang up on her.

It was a good half hour—more accurately, a bad half

hour— before she was able to concentrate on her own work again.

"Sorry," Calen said as he replaced the phone and swiveled his chair toward his visitor again.

The attractive young woman, Melissa somebody, rearranged her legs and flipped a page in her steno pad. "No problem. I really appreciate your taking time to talk to me. This is my first article for *Boulder Magazine*, so I'm probably asking more questions than I need to, but I want to be sure I don't leave anything out I might need later. If the editor likes my story about you, he says I can do a series on other men and women who serve the community."

She reminded him of Maxey. The blond hair and quick smile were part of it, but most of it was her intelligent, interested attitude. She wore a frilly peasant blouse and a splashy-flowered, billowy skirt that Maxey wouldn't have worn to anything but a Halloween party. Still, they looked good on Melissa.

Who was, no question, flirting with him. It flattered him, but mostly it made him feel fogy-old.

"Are you a native Coloradoan?" she asked.

"Right. Born in Denver."

"And did you want to be a fireman when you grew up?"

"I did."

"No little kid ever wants to be a dentist. Or a podiatrist, do they? Where do those people come from?" She laughed. "Are your parents still in Denver?"

He shook his head. He didn't think it was anybody's business that they'd both died of cancer four years ago.

Melissa kept going. "Siblings?"

"No." He didn't think it was anybody's business that his parents had often told him he was unplanned, and that they would never voluntarily take on that kind of responsibility. Bob and Jean—he'd always called them Bob and Jean—were good to him, but they were never the demonstrative, fun-loving parents he'd have chosen for himself.

He shifted in his chair, unhappy to be reminded of his less than carefree childhood.

"Married?"

"No."

"Never or not yet?" Melissa persisted, grinning as she did it.

"What's that got to do with my being an arson investigator?" Irritation roughened his voice.

"Human interest. We want to get to know the man behind the badge. What he hates, what he loves. What turns him on." Melissa actually licked her crimson lips.

"Would you like some coffee?" he asked, jumping up too fast, banging a knee on the underside of his desk.

In the break room, he took his time drawing two cups, composing himself. If he'd been the type to be unfair, he'd have blamed his whole bad day on Maxey.

As the hours wore by, activity on the downtown pedestrian mall picked up, gathering momentum for the evening's celebration of the grotesque. The city government and the mall's merchants no longer encouraged revelers to come to Pearl Street for Halloween, not since the holiday had gotten out of hand in the eighties, when thousands of party animals had jammed the four-block promenade. The concomitant problems included property damage, fights, drugs, booze, and—in the case of a few Saran Wrap costumes—indecent exposures. During the worst years, storefronts were boarded up for the holiday like eastern seaboard businesses staving off hurricanes.

Nowadays at Halloween, the stores closed early, the cops routed traffic away from downtown and enforced an eleven o'clock curfew on kids, and only diehard celebrants paraded up and down the walkways, like refugees from the *Star Wars* barroom.

At about normal quitting time, Maxey hung up the telephone with extra gentleness, because slamming it down would be a childish, if satisfying, reaction to yet another dead end in her quest for Betsy/B.J. information. Standing and stretching, she walked to the window, fists on hips, to watch uninhibited humanity stream by.

"I don't think Betsy died in any car accident," she said. "I don't think she's dead at all. B. J. is probably holding her prisoner in the basement of the Underwood house while he drains off her inheritance by sucking up to Mrs. Underwood. And Basil found out, so B. J. killed Basil, and Sylvia found out about Basil's murder, so B. J. killed her, too, and then he stole Sylvia's junk boxes from me because he thought Sylvia had written down her suspicions on a chewing gum wrapper."

"Didn't Sylvia die before Basil?" Scotty asked, shutting a file drawer with a decisive rumble and clang.

"Oh. Yeah. How do you like the theory otherwise?"

Scotty hummed a few bars of *Impossible Dream* as he buttoned up his desk. "I'll drive you home," he offered.

"No, thanks. I want to walk. I'll take the camera and shoot some of the better costumes on the way."

"Okay, then I'll *walk* you home."

"I'll be fine on my own, Scotty. Look at that mob out there. Besides, I've got a pocket full of red hot pepper spray."

"Jeeze—I guess I don't want to hang out with a woman that well-prepared," Scotty said, giving up. He bestowed a fatherly hug before he slipped out the front door.

Maxey checked that the camera contained a fresh roll of film before she shut off most of the lights and locked up. She paused after shutting the door, to get her sensory bearings.

The evening smelled of popcorn and sounded like a jungle gym, the pervasive laughter punctuated by hoots and wails and snatches of song. Maxey let Morticia and Uncle Fester glide and scuttle by before she swung into the eastbound foot traffic. She checked the camera's exposure setting and snapped a rear view of the Addamses just as lean, elegant Morticia reached out a slender, graceful hand to cup her companion's ample bottom.

"Yes," Maxey muttered, envisioning the great photo. Now this was more like it. This was why she enjoyed newspaper work.

She scanned the crowd for other Pulitzer opportunities: A green canvas caterpillar underpinned by six pairs of human legs with assorted strides; a man dressed as a bowl of red Jell-O, the dessert jiggling and dancing inside a plastic globe affair he'd strapped around his overweight, jiggling, dancing body; a devil in a blue dress; Marge Simpson.

Glad to be wearing comfortable sneakers, jeans and a sweat jacket, Maxey scrambled to get the pictures she wanted, striding ahead of costumed groups, twisting and shooting, stepping up on benches or crouching on the pavement, working her way east, running out of film well before she ran out of mall.

Crossing Fifteenth Street, she turned north. She adjusted the camera strap around her neck, replaced the lens cap, and settled into a comfortable pace that would have her home within a few minutes.

In the shadow of the Flatirons, Boulder's evening rapidly became night. Marching along an unusually traffic-free Fifteenth toward Spruce, Maxey left the mall lights behind. She could see men in reflective red vests setting up barricades at the top of the hill, to discourage revelers from reveling downtown. She turned confidently onto Spruce and kept going, but she experienced a tweak of uneasiness at the darker, quieter street lying ahead. She patted her jacket at the reassuring lump of pepper spray can in the pocket.

She suddenly couldn't remember seeing Sylvia's purple box wedged among the books on the office table today. Shoving that small worry aside, she found another one to take its place. Had she promised Ollie Kraig she'd be home before six o'clock to help with the trick-or-treaters? She angled her wrist toward a street lamp to check her watch. She began to trot, clutching the bobbing camera to her chest.

Midway up the block, she veered off to cross the street, siting both ways before running across. Her house loomed over her, the damned porch light still burned out, the porch full of shadows that swayed in the erratic wind.

Would the pulsing air know her name tonight?

Flat-out unnerved now, Maxey fumbled the pepper spray out of her pocket as she dashed up the porch steps. She rushed the length of the porch floor, and searched for her key ring in the tight front pocket of her jeans. They clinked free, spilled through her fingers and hit the floor.

She bent over to retrieve them and her front door swooped open. Yelping, Maxey fell away from it, landing hard on one elbow. The can of pepper spray popped free and rolled across the porch to drop into the bushes.

"Damn it! Calen?"

A green-gloved hand reached out and smothered her mouth. And then, like a fly invited to the spider's parlor, she was dragged headfirst into her dark stairwell.

9

The door banged shut behind them.

"No screaming," a voice muttered hoarsely out of the blackness, as what felt like half a dozen hands busily groped Maxey for a good hammerlock. "Scream and I'll give you something to scream about."

Maxey managed to whip the camera from around her neck and slam it at where she guessed a face might be, but she guessed wrong, and the momentum pitched her forward, deeper into the attacker's embrace. The camera slipped through her hand and hit the floor with an ominous crunching sound, but she didn't have time to mourn it.

Held too closely to knee any groins, she elbowed with abandon until a hard little object jabbing against her lower back claimed all her attention. She froze, expecting to explode in pain at any second, paralyzed by terror of the bullet's power to paralyze.

"Ahh," the attacker exhaled in her face. He needed a mouth wash.

Maxey whimpered. "If you shoot me, you'll shoot yourself."

They breathed hard for a while. His grip on her began to tremble in time with the shaking of her knees, and they both sank down on a stair step. The gun eased away, but before she could enjoy any relief, it burrowed into her side.

"Now then," he whispered. Having been in such close combat, Maxey had no doubt it was a "he".

"Now then," he repeated.

Maxey felt hysterical laugher bubble toward the surface. He sounded as if he'd forgotten why he'd come.

"I'll let you go, and I'll remove the pistol from your ribs, but you have to be very still and do exactly as I tell you."

"Okay," Maxey whispered, too, mentally crossing all her fingers and toes. Had she heard this voice before, engaged in more civilized conversation?

They released one another slowly, and Maxey leaned away from him. Picturing the nasty little gun in front of her now, she clenched her stomach muscles in a useless, defensive reaction.

"Now then. I want you to come with me. Don't try to call attention to us out there on the street. If you try to get help, I'll shoot you. I will shoot you."

"Where are we going? What do you want from me?" She hated how her voice shivered up and down the scale.

Of course, he didn't answer her. He scuffled up to his feet and cracked open the door to the porch and peered out for a moment. The only light came from the street lamp across Spruce, but it was enough.

Maxey stared, hysteria still tickling her throat. She'd expected to behold Jack the Ripper. Instead, she was being kidnapped by Kermit the Frog.

He squatted down to pick up her keys and tossed them inside on the floor. Then he motioned her past him out the door. "Shhh."

Maybe not Kermit, but definitely a frog. Even in the poor light, his costume glowed slime-green—padded suit, tights, webbed feet. The bug-eyed mask was a helmet that covered his head down to his upper lip. Maxey tried to recognize that chin, that mouth, that slightly pronounced philtrum.

He pushed her impatiently across the porch and herded

her toward the street. They looked both ways and waited for a pickup truck to rattle past. The driver honked and someone in the back yelled, "Ribbit, dude!"

"What would you have done if I'd had someone with me?" Maxey demanded as Swamp-breath nudged her off the curb. "I could have had a bunch of friends with me when I came home."

He grunted. "Shot them, I guess."

"You wouldn't have!"

"It's academic, so kindly shut up." His raspy wheeze gave her no clues to his identity.

He grabbed her arm to aim her toward a side yard between houses, and she found herself retracing the route she and Calen had taken the night of the Futon Lode fire, to a gate in a back fence that led to the alley behind Derrick's building.

This frog was too stocky to be Derrick, had too thick a jaw to be B. J. Underwood. He broke her chain of speculation by jerking her to a stop on the edge of the alley. He peered both ways, then back the way they'd come, and then both ways of the alley again, as if he suspected an ambush.

Maxey reconnoitered too, hoping for someone at a window who would see them and remember her when Calen and Officer Madrid came around asking questions.

Oh God.

She didn't spy a single spectator.

"Go," Swamp-thing muttered, hauling her across the alley to the small back door of the shared loading dock of Hill's Office Supply and the Futon Lode.

They stumbled against it together, he turned the knob without having to unlock it, and they blundered inside. By a single bare bulb in the center of the ceiling, Maxey could see that Derrick had begun to use the black-walled room again. It contained three green recycling barrels and one futon frame canted on a broken leg.

Swamp-gas walked Maxey to a side door in the west wall. "This way," he said in his normal voice.

She gave her head one quick shake, trying to clear it of surprise. "You? Oh, come on. What is this, Mr. Hill? Candid camera?"

Wrenching her arm out of his grasp, she backed away, embarrassed that she could have been so scared of this old man. Who would have guessed the geezer would be so strong, that he could transmute from the Gray Guppy into Superfrog? Whatever his problem was, she should have been able to get away from him before now—maybe by promising him a cream cheese Danish before karate-chopping the gun out of his slimy hand.

Sighing, he held up the pistol, well away from any sudden moves she might make. "It's not a practical joke, Ms. Burnell. This is a real gun with real bullets and I really would shoot you. If you don't want me to prove it right this minute, then please go through this door."

The little room beyond was another receiving area, but this one was cramped with cardboard cartons, tables, gray metal shelving, file cabinets—stuff. Mrs. Hill sat in a high-backed executive chair reading a newspaper—not the *Regard.* She was not in costume, unless the print dress and sensible oxfords were supposed to be somebody's grandma. Folding the paper shut, she studied Maxey, stony-faced.

"Any trouble?" she asked her husband.

He peeled the frog mask off before shaking his head. Attached to the suit, the green skull hung down the back of his neck as if he were molting.

"Did you search her?"

He shook his head again.

"Kindly turn out your pockets, Ms. Burnell," Mrs. Hill said, and she narrowed her eyes watching, as Maxey demonstrated she had no guns, no knives, no—damn it all—self defense sprays.

"This has gone far enough," Maxey said, forcing her voice into a firm, reasonable pitch. "Say what you have to say and let me go home. I'm supposed to be helping my neighbor-friend with the trick-or-treaters right now." She took a stance, spread-legged with arms folded, hoping it looked more confident than she felt.

The Hills talked across her as if she weren't there.

"We might as well begin right away, Avery. Derrick won't be back for several hours, but it's going to take us a while to get ready to leave."

"All right. Have you got everything we need here?"

"I think so. I cleared off that table."

Maxey looked at where she pointed, feeling equal parts mystified and apprehensive. The standard, six-foot metal table was, indeed, clear of everything except dust and one pair of needle-nosed pliers. Maxey didn't mind the dust, but she didn't care for the pliers.

"Okay." Mr. Hill heaved a sigh from the bottom of his lungs and gazed down at the pistol in his hand. "I hate this."

"I know, dear. I do, too."

"I do, too," Maxey added her vote. "So let's all go home and forget it."

Mrs. Hill tch tched. "You're scared, of course. Fear of the unknown is always worse than fear of the known, so let me explain this to you. We're going to—" She grimaced. "It isn't going to hurt."

"For godsake, *what* are you dithering about?"

Mrs. Hill's eyes seemed suddenly wet. "Well, Maxey, first we're going to sedate you. Then we're going to. . . do something else to you. And lastly, we'll burn down the building."

Scotty picked up the portable phone on the third ring, a cold can of Coors moistening his other hand. The television was too loud, because he'd just tuned it to Monday Night Football and hadn't had a chance to set the volume yet. He had to ask the caller to repeat himself.

"It's about Maxey. You are the gentleman who works with her at the newspaper, aren't you? I found your name on the masthead, and there was only one Scotty Springer in the telephone book."

By now, Scotty had found the remote control in the cushions of his lumpy sofa and clicked the pre-game highlights down to a grumble. "Yes. Who's calling?"

"Ollie Kraig. I live downstairs from Maxey."

"Right. What's the problem, sir?"

"I'm a little concerned about her. We had an arrangement where she was to help me with the children begging for treats tonight. She hasn't come, but her car is parked up the street a ways. I know she sometimes walks to work, so I'd have thought she's just a bit late getting home, except the porch light is burned out, so I got the step stool out and put in a new bulb, and then, once there was some illumination, I noticed that her door onto the porch wasn't quite shut."

Scotty tapped the television sound completely off. "Are there any lights in her apartment?"

"Not that I can see. I called up the stairs—which are dark, by the way—and got no answer. I don't want to be a busybody, but after the other night when someone attacked her out by the garage, I can't help being concerned."

"I appreciate that. Let me see if I can track her down."

"She's not at the office. I tried calling there. I also tried her home number and got the answering machine."

"Okay. Let me do some checking and get back to you. If you see her first, give me a ring. I might be at a different phone." Scotty recited his cellular phone number.

"I hope she's just forgotten our date," Ollie Kraig said. "I do hope she's just being a pain in the ass."

Scotty's chuckle was automatic as he stabbed the reset button and dialed the office to double check that Maxey wasn't there. While he listened to ten rings, he consulted his flip-up list directory to refresh his memory on Calen Taylor's home number. Giving up on the *Regard*, he tapped more buttons on the telephone.

When Calen answered, Scotty could hear the sound of a razor blade commercial that matched the picture on Scotty's television set.

"Is Maxey there?" he asked without preamble.

"Scotty?"

"Right. She's not there, is she?"

"No. What's the trouble?"

"I've temporarily misplaced her. I thought she was leaving the office right after I did about an hour ago, but Ollie Kraig says she's not at home. But her car's there and her front door's ajar."

"Damn."

"Yeah."

"She was planning to stay in tonight and greet the trick-or-treaters."

"She was. I'm going to drive back to the office." Scotty reached for the denim jacket he'd tossed on the back of the couch. "Maybe she's just not answering the phone. Let me give you my cellular number, in case."

"I'll start at the other end. I've got a key to the door upstairs. Could be she fell asleep up there. We're probably getting excited about nothing. But damn, I knew I should have picked her up at work."

Maxey's heart wasn't racing and blood wasn't thundering in her ears in reaction to her fright. Rather, she felt leaden and numb and slow-witted. Why did these two crazy geriatrics want to be the death of her?

Her mouth still worked. "What's going on?"

"Oh, it's too long a story." Mrs. Hill waved away the question.

"Come on, tell me. We're waiting for Derrick anyway. Right?"

"I'm tired," Mr. Hill said, pulling a stool out from under another table, dragging it in front of the door he'd been guarding, and easing down on it. His forehead glistened with sweat. He began to peel off the frog suit in an effortful, one-handed struggle, a molecule at a time. The pistol weaved in his other hand, most of the time aimed toward Maxey and some of the time aimed at his wife.

"Come on. Talk to me," Maxey repeated, fighting the

impulse to scream it.

Mrs. Hill shrugged. "I've already told you. We can't find a buyer for the store, and we simply must retire before it's too late. Before we're in wheelchairs or worse."

"You're sick." Maxey didn't ask it; she considered it an accurate description.

"No, no." Mrs. Hill shook her head, irritated. "We're old. Getting older. Like the song says, the days come down to priceless few. We don't want to kick off in the middle of selling a Bic pen and a ream of typing paper. I want to see Hawaii. I want to sleep late Saturday mornings. I want to tell two or three of our precious customers to go to hell."

"You set the fire that killed Basil," Maxey guessed.

Not only did the Hills scare her, it scared her that her adrenaline supply seemed to have run out, leaving her as listless as Mr. Hill usually looked. She hoped her body knew what it was doing—perhaps storing up energy for a break to freedom that would surprise her as much as it surprised the opposition.

"It was an accident," Mrs. Hill said. "How were we to know he'd be in the building? There'd never been anyone in the building that late before."

"Why not have a liquidation sale?" Maxey demanded. "Close out the business? Surely the inventory and fixtures would finance a trip to Honolulu."

"Avery figured it up. There's more money and a lot less hassle in collecting fire insurance."

"Not if you murder someone! That's a monumental hassle, especially for the victim!"

"It wasn't murder," Mrs. Hill shouted down Maxey.

"What do you call what you plan for me?" Maxey shouted back.

Mr. Hill stumbled up, waving the gun. "Don't let her upset you, Hester. Get the ether and let's have this thing over with."

"No, wait." Maxey held up a hand. "I'm sorry. Of course Basil was an accident. You must have been horrified when you heard the news."

"Oh, we were," Mrs. Hill said, her voice again quietly conversational, and Avery resettled on his stool. "Then on top of that, here came your newspaper article telling about Sylvia and her wretched boxes of personal effects."

"Sylvia." Maxey needed to sit down, but the Hills had all the chairs. Under different circumstances, she would have perched herself on the bare table, but that didn't seem advisable right now. "Sylvia?"

"There, you see, Hester, she hasn't figured it out." Avery rearranged his legs with an impatient flounce. "You were worried about nothing."

"Perhaps she hasn't figured it out yet, but she would have sooner or later, you can wager on that. Anyway, we want to take advantage of the $100,000 accidental death policy, don't we?"

Maxey absolutely, positively had to sit down. She settled for cross-legged on the floor. It wasn't the readiest of positions in case she needed to counterattack. However, it was better than passing out flat, especially since the latter was apparently the position the Hills wanted her to assume.

"What hundred thousand accidental death policy?" she asked, leaning her back against the table leg.

"Both Avery and I have policies. Have had them for years, so it won't seem suspicious now. We got the idea from Basil, actually. Derrick said he was burned beyond recognition, but of course dental records would confirm it was his body. So we're going to kill two birds here, if you'll excuse a cliche´. We're going to collect the money for our ruined business, and we're going to collect the money for my accidental death. I was working late, you see."

Maxey saw, but she very much wished she couldn't.

Mrs. Hill smiled gently. "You will be me. And then you won't keep stirring up the Sylvia thing."

Maxey shook her head. "I have dental records, too."

"And so do I." Mrs. Hill jutted her jaw and her lower teeth lurched up into her mouth. She pushed them down manually and smacked her lips. "Dentures," she said with satisfaction.

On a wave of panic, Maxey squeezed shut her eyes, but she could still see the needle-nosed pliers.

As soon as he stepped inside the *Regard* office, Scotty knew Maxey wasn't in it. Nevertheless, he called her name, listened, and then walked from the front toward the back checking out all the nooks and crannies she might fit into under extraordinary circumstances. The telephone rang, and he ducked as if he'd been shot at.

He grabbed up the receiver. "Yes?"

"She's not here at the apartment," Calen said. "According to Moe, she never came home to feed him supper."

"She's not in the office either."

"Something else that doesn't look too good to me—she left her camera and her keys on the floor of the vestibule, down by the street door."

"No—doesn't sound like Maxey. What do you want to do next?"

"There were two guys she suspected of that attack behind the house the other night. You know who I mean?"

Scotty pinched the bridge of his nose to think. "Robert Whatshisname and B. J. Underwood."

"Sounds right. You want to take one and I'll take the other?"

"I'll hunt up Robert. I know what he looks like and where he lives. I'm pretty sure you'll find a listing for Underwood in the phone book."

"Scotty, if anything seems the least bit off, call in the police."

"At the moment, I'm looking out the window at a six-foot penguin in jockey shorts."

"Use your best judgment."

Scotty replaced the telephone, locked up, and headed out to collect the Bronco he'd had to park five blocks away.

***

"What did Sylvia do to you?" Maxey asked, turning from Hill to Hill. "What would I have discovered if I'd kept digging into her life?" Or her death, as the case might be.

Husband and wife exchanged a look.

"We thought she might have stolen something from us," Mrs. Hill said. "That's all."

Maxey snorted. "What? A rubber band?" She was startled to see them exchange that look again. "I thought I was kidding, but—a rubber band?"

"I told you she'd catch on eventually," Avery Hill said.

Maxey longed to shake him. "Catch on to what?"

"Shh, listen!"

Everyone held his or her breath. The sound Mrs. Hill had heard repeated itself—a passerby beating the front window with a fist.

"Kids!" she said. "They do that all the time. Someday the glass is going to break and slice an arm off." She consulted her wristwatch. "Is it really only half past seven?"

"You two burglarized my apartment? You took Sylvia's boxes? Looking for a rubber band?"

"Just Avery. I'm not good at climbing stairs anymore, thanks to this darned arthritis. He's excellent with locks. His daddy was a locksmith."

"How did you know where I live?"

"You're in the phone book, of course. Imagine our surprise when we found you lived right behind us here. Avery made a dry run first, knocking at the door with a delivery of yellow legal pads. But it was a Mr. Kraig who answered and said that you lived upstairs and pointed out your door."

Avery chuckled here, a throat-clearing eruption of amusement that verged on a choke. "I went to school with Ollie Kraig. I didn't know that he lived behind us either. He didn't realize that Hill's Office Supply was me. We're going to get together for dinner sometime. After I retire."

"There, you see?" Mrs Hill said, smiling fondly his direction. "Something else to look forward to once the store is gone."

Another tactless remark, Maxey thought, considering how little *she* had to look forward to. "How'd you know the boxes were at my apartment?"

"We didn't. But they were, weren't they?" Mrs. H. said smugly.

"So Avery skulked back another time, violated the lock on my door, wormed upstairs, and sleazed off with Sylvia's— now my— belongings. And did you find the rubber band?"

Mrs. Hill's expression of pride over her husband's ability to break and enter faded into an expression of regret. "Probably not. They all tend to look alike, you know."

The woman was driving Maxey toward a fit of the screaming-meemies. With titanic effort, she swallowed them back. "Did either or both of you have anything to do with Sylvia plummeting down the stairs?"

"Gracious, but you ask bald-faced questions. A regular Barbara Walters," Mrs. Hill said.

"It was an accident," Mr. Hill said.

Maxey restrained herself from commenting on their accident-proneness.

"I went to her rooming house in an attempt to talk her into returning our property," he continued.

"The rubber band," Maxey said.

"She was most uncooperative. So I picked up the blue cigar box that was right there in plain sight and started down the hall with it, to sort through at my leisure."

"And to return the same way, of course," Mrs. Hill interjected.

"But she chased after me, and tried to push me down the steps. Of course, I reflexively moved aside, and she was the one to go teakettle over spout. Although no one else was in the hall, I knew there were people in the building who could attend to her injuries, so I hurried on outside and home. Unfortunately, after all my trouble, there was nothing of value in that box."

"You learned from my newspaper article that Sylvia had two other boxes."

"We should have guessed," Mrs. Hill mildly reproached her husband. "A pack rat never throws anything away."

Maxey squirmed to a less uncomfortable position on the hard tile floor. Now would be the logical time for her to mention that Sylvia had possessed yet another, fourth, box. But somehow that purple box felt like the lone tool in an inadequate survival kit, and she clamped the secret of its existence between her still strongly rooted teeth.

10

Robert Truet didn't seem to be at home. Scotty rattled the doorknob, squinted appraisingly at the framework, stepped back leg's length, and gave the door one swift kick. It burst open and Scotty ambled inside. Nobody came to investigate the crash. The crime was probably one of a long list perpetrated and ignored at the Bluebell House on an average day.

He found the overhead light switch, which upgraded the unoccupied room from dim to semi-dim. Pads of paper and loose pages, covered with scrawled words, littered every horizontal surface—sofa, table, kitchen counter, bed, floor. Robert/Roberto was a poem machine.

Scotty backed out of the room and shut the door. The latch seemed only a little worse for wear. Next, he checked out the communal men's bathroom up the hall, where the decor relied heavily on chipped porcelain and exposed pipes. The only person there, installed in a stall, had legs way too dark to be Robert's.

"Did either of you happen to throw my clothes in my boyfriend's dryer last Saturday?"

The Hills stared at Maxey as if she were the crazy one here.

"Okay, what about Friday night at the garage behind

my house? That was you in the vampire get-up right, Avery?"

He frowned, as if trying to recall, before shaking his head. He shuffled his feet, preparing to stand.

"Let me ask you something else," Maxey rushed to distract him. "What does B. J. Underwood have to do with all of this?"

"You mean the typewriter?" Mrs. Hill looked doubtful. "We don't sell typewriters."

"Basil's cousin. The second face you helped me photocopy this morning."

"Don't know him," the Hills said in unison.

"I'm looking for B. J. Underwood," Calen said to the young man with the dark, tousled hair, the seven o'clock shadow, and the pear-shaped build. "I think I've found him."

"Why do you think that?" He asked it without belligerence, with mild curiosity and also mild resignation.

"I've seen a drawing of you. Maxey wanted to add fangs to it."

"Figures. Come in."

Since this wasn't the reception Calen expected, he hesitated.

"Come in, come in." The man beckoned with all his fingers. "We'll have to talk in the kitchen because Mom will be busy here at the front distributing candy to the hordes."

Calen stepped into the little house and glanced to his right, where a huge, white-skinned woman in a splashy flowered-print caftan sat on the edge of a couch, hugging a stainless steel bowl heaped with midget-sized Mars bars. She smiled and Calen nodded.

"In here," B. J. said, walking through an archway, through a dining room, into a kitchen. It all felt unpleasantly cramped—small rooms, large furniture. His guide turned ample hips sideways to negotiate the narrows. Calen couldn't imagine the heavyset lady moving around in here at all.

B. J. motioned at the round, white-painted table, and they sat down on opposite sides, eying one another like arm wrestlers about to lock fists.

"I'm looking for Maxey," Calen started to say at the same moment that B. J. said, "I guess I'm screwed."

"Now, Maxey, I have to apologize. This isn't real ether. I just didn't know where to go to get that."

While Mrs. Hill rummaged in a desk drawer, Maxey scrabbled to her knees and Avery Hill stood up.

"There was this book at the public library that told about household chemicals, and it said some lighter fluids contain ether. This one—" She brought a little yellow and blue can triumphantly into the light. "This one doesn't say anything about ether, but it has napthas, which the book says causes narcosis, so it should be just as good. Don't you think? Now what we need is a good, clean rag." She opened a storage cabinet door and rooted again.

"I thought you said you were all ready," Avery complained.

"Well, I am. It's all here, Mr. Can't-Hold-My-Britches," his helpmate sniped back.

Maxey staggered to her feet. Avery pointed the gun at her chest, two-handed, arms straight, and appeared to be trying to remember the command for "hold still."

Maxey swayed, dredging up words of her own. "Wait. It's early yet. I want to know how you talked Derrick into this. I'd never have believed he would. . . . What does he gain?"

Mrs. Hill dangled a bit of white cheesecloth for Avery to admire. "Derrick doesn't gain anything. In fact, he may very well lose his life if he doesn't work fast tonight. Once we set the delay device, he has a maximum of one hour to clean up his side and get out. I don't give him very good odds."

It was in Maxey's best interest to keep the old lady talking, even if she talked like the Mad Hatter. "Clean up his side?"

"We told him we would supply him with some wonderful stuff that a fireman friend recommended for taking the smoke stink out of his store. I got the name out of that same library book—amyl acetate. We told him it smells like bananas, which it very well may. And we told him to be careful, because it's flammable, which it is. Especially—" Here Mrs. Hill grinned across the room at her husband and he twitched a quick smile in response. "—Since what we really gave him in those big gallon containers is kerosene."

"You're going to murder a young father so you can loll around the beach for the rest of your miserable lives?" Maxey blurted.

"Oh, he may be fine. It depends on whether he wastes any time wiping down the walls and floor with the kerosene before the fire starts in earnest. If he's still in the building when the whole thing goes up, he might get out, even then. In any event, too bad for him, he'll be the one blamed for arson."

"But he'll tell everyone it was you who supplied him with the accelerant."

"Pooh. His word against Avery's. A grieving Avery, who'll have everyone's sympathy because he's just lost his wife of forty-three wonderful years."

"I assume you have a bunker to hide out in, Hester?" Maxey snarled. "Cooling your heels, excuse the expression, till the heat, excuse the expression, is off?"

"Oh, yes, it's all taken care of. I'll be in Las Vegas, living as Ruth Delany. I had great fun picking out an alias." She held up the white cloth in one hand and the lighter fluid can in the other. "Shall we, Avery?"

At that moment, Maxey's mind underwent a miraculous transformation, from mush to Mensa. The Hills would not really shoot her, because they didn't want this to look like murder. And Avery certainly couldn't shoot her if his wife was in the line of fire.

Maxey jumped at Mrs. Hill like an uninhibited dog greeting a long-lost friend. The woman would have been bowled off her feet, except Maxey hugged her upright and twisted them both around, putting Mrs. Hill's ample back to Avery and the gun. Still clutching the can and the rag, Mrs. H. emitted shrill little bleeps of distress.

Before either Hill could gather what wits he or she yet possessed, Maxey shoved the woman away in the direction of the man and ducked out the door into the dark office supply showroom.

She raced flat out toward the front of the building along an invisible center aisle she hoped was free of vacuum cleaners and other booby traps. Back in the bowels of the building, Mrs. Hill screeched, "What's the matter with you? What's the matter with you?" but whether she meant Maxey or Avery wasn't apparent.

Maxey hit the front door hard, as if she'd been dropped from a height on it—palms, knees, chin, and chest. Rebounding, she launched herself against it again, pushing at the bar across the center. But it was only a handle, not a release mechanism. The door was tightly locked and she was trapped, so she indulged herself in a throat-scraping scream. As she pounded on the glass and drew breath for the next shriek, a trio of kids in regulation grunge-wear shuffled to a dead stop on the sidewalk to stare in at her.

"Help," she shouted. "Call 911!"

The three boys froze in place, faces blank or frowning. Then the one with the backwards baseball cap broke into a comprehending grin.

"Cool effects, lady!"

The other two exchanged looks and then they, too, relaxed. "Whooo," one voiced, shaking his upraised hands like a rap singer. The third kid pointed at the show window to the west.

"The skeletons are pretty lame," he called. "Need a ton of ketchup smeared around or something."

"No, wait!" Maxey could hardly hear them laughing through the heavy glass as they bobbed on up the street.

Behind her, she clearly heard the Hills moving purposefully through the showroom. The realization came way too late that she should have held Mrs. Hill hostage and gone out the back door, marched the woman up the alley beyond Avery's range, turned her loose, and run like hell. No use crying over spilt opportunities.

She took a fistful of show window drapery and yanked it out of the way, leaping in among the skeletons, sending them into a clicking, spinning frenzy. Wishing she were wearing ski boots instead of canvas sneakers, she kicked at the plate glass that Mrs. Hill had proclaimed so vulnerable.

Like much of what Mrs. Hill said, this turned out to be nonsense. The window shuddered and held, even when Maxey grabbed a secretarial chair and rammed it.

"Ms. Burnell," Avery Hill scolded from much too close.

Glimpsing his shadowy shape to her left, Maxey ran right, fought her way through the drapery and stumbled into the dark of the main room again. Arms outstretched, she came up short against a merchandise gondola. She groped it wildly, hoping for scissors, letter knives, even a sharp ballpoint pen, but finding only flimsy packs of paper.

"Ms. Burnell, you are only prolonging the inevitable," Avery said from an aisle or two away.

She felt her way to the next row of shelves: Tape dispensers, postage scales, rubber fingers, something that felt like a canister of pepper spray but was probably only spray-on glue. She took a can with her, just in case.

"I've disconnected the phones," Mrs. Hill's high, sour voice announced into the dark.

Liar, Maxey thought. *Liar, liar, pants on fi. . . .* She hastily shifted mental gears, trying to guess where the phones would be. Check-out desk. Office. Shipping-receiving, though she hadn't seen one there. Basement—was there a basement? Mezzanine. Mrs. H. couldn't manage stairs very well, she'd said.

Crouching low and trying to be quiet about bumping into things, Maxey headed for the steps to the upstairs. When she finally found them, they were broad and shallow and made of marble so they didn't squeak. She tiptoed up, guided by the tight grip she kept on the banister. At the top, she slid her feet along the carpet in short jerks of exploratory forward progress.

The dark mezzanine didn't seem to have any logical aisles. A jumble of chairs and desks, it was a nightmare maze of hard edges at shin and thigh height. Trying to hurry and yet keep quiet while colliding with large objects that either rolled or didn't yield in the slightest took its toll on her breath and her soft parts. There wasn't even a red exit sign to be seen. *Especially* there wasn't a red exit sign to be seen.

She worked her way toward the rear, where a faint suck and slap seemed to indicate a window blind on a leaky window overlooking the alley. Below and behind her, the Hills quarreled back and forth about what to do next to corral her.

She smelled synthetic pine, the kind that's supposed to improve the ambiance of a public restroom. Stubbing her knee on a metal cabinet, she cringed at the tiny gong of alarm it issued. Circling it, she touched a wall and followed that to an alcove where the sound of the blind ebbed louder. Hands outstretched, she shuffled into the space, caught the struggling canvas and lifted it up.

Light from a lamp in the alley filtered through the louvers of a ventilator. No window.

Holding the blind aloft, she craned over each shoulder, inspecting her surroundings by the inadequate illumination. On her right, a restroom door stood open on a blackness full of, apparently, evergreen trees. On her left, an old-fashioned freight elevator slept behind protective grillwork. For a few seconds she considered taking it. She could keep pushing buttons, ride from floor to floor all night, till the Hills had to give up because it was time to open the store and eat donuts.

But they could still set the building on fire, and an elevator cage was the last place she'd want to be.

She listened to the hushed building, imagining other ears listening, too. She looked down at the can she'd grabbed from the display downstairs, still clamped in one fist. Compressed Air Computer Duster, it said. $9.99.

Maxey shook her head, mildly scandalized at the price of high technology. She lowered the blind with regret, extinguishing that little semblance of light, to continue her search for escape—a back stair exit, perhaps? Her eyes needed to readjust to the blackness. She shut them and waited, longing to go to sleep and wake up in her own bed.

Rustling below-stairs got her moving again. She skirted where she pictured the blabbermouth metal cabinet to be and put out her empty left hand to help her trail the back wall around. It felt chalk-dry and dusty. Now and again she'd detour across a pockmarked pegboard or a cardboard carton lean-to.

Any moment she expected to touch a doorframe. When she didn't, when she came to the corner and had to shunt toward the front of the mezzanine again, she told herself it would be here, on this side wall. Please.

But all she encountered was more furniture and a display of something small, clocks perhaps, that fell away from her and clatter-rattled off in all directions.

No longer hampered by the restrictions of stealth, she stumbled and thumped the length of that wall without finding any doors or telephones. When she fetched up against the mezzanine railing, she followed it to the right, though it wasn't going to lead where she wanted to go.

She drifted to a stop and swayed out to look over the edge. Enough light filtered into the showroom from the rear and from the front street to show her Mr. Hill standing directly below, hands on hips, his pale, featureless face turned up at her. A lion, waiting for the Christian.

"B. J. is Betsy. Or more accurately, Betsy is now B. J." Calen peered out the side window of Scotty's Bronco, yearning for Maxey to materialize on the indistinct sidewalk.

"A transvestite?" Scotty asked, watching out his own side, driving slow.

"No, a transsexual."

"I guess I don't know the difference."

"A transsexual isn't content to dress up in the clothes of the opposite sex. He or she takes hormones and undergoes surgery to actually become the other sex."

Scotty grunted.

"It takes place by steps. The biological female takes androgens, which grow hair on her face. They also change the distribution of body fat so shoulders get broader and the rest of the torso gets more male-like. Her vocal chords thicken so she talks lower. She stops having menstrual periods. If she wants to go the whole route, there's mastectomy and hysterectomy. Nowadays there's even a way a surgeon can construct male genitalia."

Scotty grunted again. "She—B. J. told you all this?"

"Right. Damn, it was all so extraordinary, I forgot I was in a hurry. But I guess I wasn't there more than fifteen minutes. He didn't waste any words."

"And you're satisfied he didn't know anything about Maxey's disappearance?"

"He let me search the house. Of course, he could have already done something with her. But I don't think so. I believe B. J. threatened Maxey solely because he didn't want it widely known that he'd undergone gender reconstruction."

"Is that what B. J. called it?"

"Sure, what would you call it?"

"Painful. In every goddamn way."

Calen huffed a sigh, glad his impression of Scotty as a broad-minded old cuss was correct. "Betsy left Colorado a woman, came back from California a man. A new man, you might say. A different name, a fresh start, a good job. You can't blame him for being nervous when Maxey started in on him and his mom."

"Did you tell him that all he needed to do was tell Maxey the truth and she'd have left him alone?"

"Would she have? B. J. could still be up to no good. He could have murdered Basil, for whatever reason."

If that was the case, Scotty thought Maxey might be

beyond their reach. He rummaged in his mental file of favorite quotations. "John Lubbock, 1803 to 1865," he said. "'It is certainly wrong to despair; and if despair is wrong, hope is right.'"

"Yeah," Calen said without enthusiasm, distracted by a van that cut in front of them.

Scotty kept the next saying to himself, the one by Norman Cousins: "Hope is independent of the apparatus of logic."

"Maxey Burnell, where are you! If you don't come out right this minute, we aren't going to have time to asphyxiate you and pull your teeth. We'll just have to knock them out with a crow bar. And don't think I don't have a crow bar, because I do."

Cowering behind a half-wall at the top of the mezzanine stairs, Maxey believed Mrs. Hill this time. If the clang of metal against banister was not a pry bar, it was something just as intimidating.

"I don't know why we have to worry about the teeth anyway," Avery grumbled, his voice deliberate and loud up the stairwell. "The human body is ninety-five per cent water. Once the fire's hot enough, her head will explode."

Maxey pressed tighter to her hiding place. After a few moments, her nausea subsided. She drew deep, deliberate breaths and felt the oxygen clear away her panic. While she regretted having rushed headlong into the equivalent of a box canyon, she wasn't waving any white flags yet.

Mrs. Hill harangued from the bottom of the stairs. Mr. Hill's plodding footsteps climbed them. He carried a flashlight that danced and bobbed, higher and higher.

Making up her mind, Maxey squirmed into a more ready position. She hated to push an old man down a flight of marble steps, but it was him or her. She waited, remembering that poor Sylvia had tried and failed to do this very thing.

I'm younger. I'm smarter. I'm prepared.

She held the can of pricey air like a truncated ball bat,

back behind her waist, ready to swing at his legs the minute they came into reach.

He stopped short of the top step. Maxey could tell by his labored breathing he was too far away to swing at.

He came up one more riser and swept the light across the mezzanine. Primed to move, Maxey lunged upward too soon and struck with the can, but he was still too far away, and she succeeded only in jarring the flashlight out of his grip. It spun on the floor, a weak strobe light that picked out carpet fiber and chair legs and Maxey's fingers, trying to lever her backward into position for another attack.

She felt as slow as a dream. In the revolving light, she glimpsed the red stick before it connected with the side of her head. Slumped against the half-wall, fighting to stay conscious, she gazed up at Avery gazing down.

It was, indeed, a crow bar.

11

Scotty and Calen bumped slowly down the alley in the Bronco. Behind the Futon Lode/Office Supply, they braked long enough to see and hear nothing unusual. A Hill's Office Supply delivery van sat in the gravel lot.

Circling the block to the front, Scotty double-parked across Pearl Street. "Where else?" he asked after a moment or two.

"Did Ollie Kraig check the back yard and the garage?"

Scotty glanced at Calen's bleak face. "Probably not."

He eased the Bronco forward to the corner and negotiated the north turn toward Spruce. One of Boulder's ubiquitous bike riders sailed by from the opposite direction, his reflective spokes like spinning fire.

Maxey blamed the film of tears in her eyes on how much her head was hurting. She wasn't to the point of giving up yet. No. But it was hard to plot and plan escape with a headache the size of Mount Massive. She sat in the receiving room on the damned six-foot table, wrists bound in front of her with enough masking tape to mail her to Pittsburgh. She remembered awareness fading in and out like a weak radio station as Mr. Hill walked her down the stairs and taped her up.

Now the Hills huddled near the door to the showroom,

settling the finer details of her fate.

"Derrick will be here any minute now. You'd better tape her mouth shut, too," Hester Hill said.

"How can you pull or push out her teeth if I tape her mouth shut?" Avery Hill said. "Why can't I just use this for the anesthetic?" He held up the crow bar.

"Because I went to the trouble of buying the lighter fluid, and I hate to let it go to waste."

"I'm not going gently," Maxey said to herself, and then louder. "I'm not going gently."

Scotty and Calen wandered aimlessly around the *Regard* office, shoulders slumped, out of good ideas. Calen stopped at Maxey's desk and searched it one more time for a clue—a jotted note, a phone number on a scrap of paper, a business card, anything. But there was nothing.

"Maybe this isn't related to the Underwoods or Sylvia Wellman at all," Scotty said, scrubbing at his face with his knuckles. "What about an old grudge? An enemy that's simmered for a while?"

"That's possible. Or it could be a random crazy who just picked her off the street. What isn't possible is that she's not in trouble. She didn't just decide to run to the mall for a new lipstick. We aren't going to be pissed off at her tomorrow for being thoughtlessly stupid tonight." Calen sat down hard in her chair.

Scotty planted his backside on the long worktable and swung his legs. He looked idly the length of it. The purple box caught his eye and he stretched to pull it out. "Did you know we found another of Sylvia's boxes?"

"Yeah. No. I'm not sure."

Scotty opened the lid and gently shook the contents.

"You know the one person who could make Maxey forget everything else, run off without telling us?" Calen said. "Her dad. What if he dropped in on her, all the way from Wyoming, completely by surprise, and took her out for dinner?"

Scotty shook his head. "She'd have called Ollie." He

pinched a piece of ruled yellow paper out of the box and shook the folds open. "She's not some dipsy bimbo."

"Yeah. I know that. What have you got there?"

"Nothing. Blank." Scotty dropped the paper beside him on the table and lifted out an almost whole cigarette. He looked at the blackened end before discarding the scarcely smoked butt next to the yellow paper.

Using his heels, Calen walked the castered chair over to the table and watched as Scotty found a hot pink paper clip and put it beside the cigarette. Calen jerked the box out of his hands, set it in his lap, and sorted through it like a dog with a bone to bury. He yanked out a book of matches.

Scotty, intrigued by Calen's sudden intensity, glimpsed *Dilly Delicatessen* printed on the cover before Calen thumbed the book open, displaying two full ranks of matches. Dropping the book on the floor, Calen stirred the box again, muttered, "Yes," and drew out three unused kitchen matches, one at a time, and laid them carefully beside the cigarette. He brushed the pink paper clip off the table, dug into the box one more time, and held up a thin, brown rubber band tangled around a white barrette.

Freeing the rubber band, Calen tossed the barrette after the rejected paper clip, onto the floor. Scotty frowned, annoyed to be so baffled by a handful of junk.

Standing, Calen set the purple box off to one side of the table and reached for the cigarette. Scotty watched him assemble the three matches around the cigarette and fasten them together with the rubber band. When he wrapped the yellow paper around the little bundle, old creases in the paper fit the contours of the matches/cigarette.

Calen handed the little package to Scotty. "Delayed incendiary device. The arsonist lights the cigarette, slips the device down into a sofa. The cigarette smolders down to the match heads, the fire takes off, and the setter can be miles away."

Scotty's stomach roiled with sudden acid. "Sylvia found

this. When she didn't tell the police about it, the arsonist tried again."

Calen was already halfway to the front door. "You take the Bronco and hunt up Derrick Sike's house. I'll run to the Futon Lode. Call the police from your cell phone. Hell, it wouldn't hurt to call the fire de—" He was out the door, dodging a human pin cushion, sprinting east.

"You see we have this neat little delay device," Mrs. Hill said as she opened the lighter fluid can and tipped it up twice, three times into the white cheesecloth. "The other two attempts, we hid it in one of Derrick's futons. Only this time, we're going to put it in my executive desk chair, because of course we want to be sure the office burns thoroughly. We learned how to make it from a PBS documentary. It's quite foolproof and almost impossible for investigators to detect."

She lifted the rag near her nose and sniffed cautiously. Shaking her head, she gave the cloth two more dollops of fluid.

"That's what Sylvia found that belonged to us—a neat little arson starter tucked into Derrick's futon," she chattered on. "Now where did I put the cap to this can?"

Maxey rubbed at her forehead with the sides of her bound hands. "When Sylvia didn't turn it in to the police, you decided it was safe to try again." She was no longer much interested in the details, but talking meant she wasn't dead yet. "You made another fire starter thing the night you murdered Basil in ice cold blood."

Mrs. Hill ignored Maxey's phrasing and smiled as she pulled the missing cap out of her dress pocket. "Okay now. So." She hovered with the lighter-fluid-drenched rag, obviously nervous about touching Maxey, like a farm wife approaching her first chicken beheading.

Mr. Hill grasped Maxey's wrists and threw a heavy thigh across her knees.

"Wait—wait! There's another box. A purple box. I

have another Sylvia box."

The light fixture in the ceiling behind Avery Hill's head drilled into Maxey's eyes. His grip on her tightened as he twisted to look at his wife. "Do you believe that?"

Hester Hill shrugged. "Do we care at this point?"

"Yes, of course you care," Maxey wailed. "You broke into my house to get it. You killed Sylvia for it. It must have the arson materials in it. They have your fingerprints on them."

"Where is this box?" Avery interjected.

"I'll take you to it."

"If it isn't at her apartment, it's at her office. We can find it later. Come on, Avery. She's just stalling." Clamping her mouth in a determined seal, Mrs. Hill stepped forward.

Mr. Hill crushed the backs of Maxey's knees against the edge of the table, and Maxey's anger reached the point of no return. She would rise up and toss him off. She would kick and scream and bite and throw things and be an all-around Tasmanian devil. She didn't know what had become of the ugly black gun, but the ugly red crow bar lay on the desk behind Hester Hill. Maxey didn't look at it. She would give no warning. Young and strong and *angry*, she would fight her way to it, snatch it up and swing and swing.

Calen raced through Halloween revelers, end-running around most of them, apologizing, "Sorry," to the ones he bumped, finding running room across Fourteenth Street, stalling impatiently behind a many-legged caterpillar that blocked the sidewalk in consultation with all its members. He sleeved away the chill of perspiration evaporating on his forehead and pushed past the green larva, stepping on some toes and eliciting some muffled curses.

Bursting through to the other side, he found twenty yards of clear running room and accelerated into it.

While he talked to the dispatcher at 911, Scotty ran his

finger down the page of the phone book to Sikes, Derrick. As soon as he could disconnect, he dialed again. He didn't think it would hurt to see who answered the phone at Derrick's house.

It was a woman.

"Could I speak to Derrick?" Scotty asked.

If she said, "Just a minute," Scotty figured he'd hang up, run for the Bronco, and drive like hell into north Boulder where Sikes lived.

"He isn't here. He's at the store. Who is this?"

Scotty hung up. He didn't think the missus was lying, though of course she might be. She might be the Bonnie to Derrick's Clyde. For the kids' sake, he hoped not.

Locking up the office, he swung left, following Calen's route the length of the pedestrian mall, not as fast a runner, but just as determined to beat his own best time.

Calen hurtled across Fifteenth Street without bothering to check for traffic. His goal in sight halfway up the block, he poured on an extra burst of speed that carried him several steps past the entry to the Futon Lode. He cupped his hands around his eyes and leaned into the plate glass show window. One overhead fluorescent fixture near the back revealed no one inside, no movement among the rows of futons.

Calen attacked the locked front door, hammering it with both fists and shouting. After a few seconds of this futility, he shoved himself away and ran the way he'd come, to circle around to the alley.

Scotty was doing fine, not even breathing hard, until he zigged when he should have zagged and hit the broad side of a monstrous caterpillar. Amidst the sound of ripping and grunting, Scotty fell into the center of a billowing green pileup of bodies. Not careful of where he put his hands or feet, he scrambled out of the thick of things and resumed his race.

There was no shortcut between buildings, through to the

alley. Calen had to go all the way to Fifteenth, cut north, and turn into the alley from that direction. As he approached the rear of the futon store, his hopes spiraled downward. The only vehicle parked there, a panel van, bore the Hill's Office Supply name. He and Scotty had seen it earlier in the same spot.

Slowing to a walk, trying to control his breathing, he wondered if he'd heard the distant cry of a siren. The wind blew the whisper of sound away.

He tried the smaller back door. It wasn't locked.

Calen stared at the knob in his hand and then at the dark gap that widened as he pulled, both thankful and horrified at this possible confirmation that his hunch had been right about Derrick and Sylvia and the arson device.

The door creaked open as far as it would go and Calen felt the wall inside, searching for a light. Before he could succeed or fail, an engine growled and headlights came bobbing up the alley. Calen backed out of the doorway and shielded his eyes, expecting the police.

Instead, a tan Dodge sedan rocked to a sudden stop yards away, the driver's door jerked open, and a voice accosted him. "Hey! What the hell do you think you're doing?" A skinny blond guy half jumped, half fell out of the car. Hands on hips, he glared at Calen.

"Derrick Sikes?"

"Yeah? Who are you?"

"Calen Taylor. Boulder Fire Department."

Derrick visibly relaxed, though he stayed in reach of his car door. "Yeah, I remember you. What are you doing?"

"I was walking up the alley here, and I noticed your back door is open."

"Well, damn. No kidding? I must have forgot to lock it after closing. Or maybe the Hills did. We're all getting older and more forgetful every day, you know."

"Lucky you came back," Calen said, strolling toward the Dodge, keeping an eye on Derrick's hands. "How'd that happen?"

"I'm going to do some clean-up. Avery Hill got me this stuff that's supposed to be good for taking the smoke odor out of the building."

"Is that right?"

By now Calen could see into the front seat, empty of anything except a child-sized pink ski jacket. He eased past Derrick and casually glanced into the back seat. It was full of the debris a family car accumulates—books, empty soda cans, flattened potato chip bags, and not one kidnapped newspaperwoman.

"I'd like to ask you a few more questions while you work," Calen said, resting his knuckles on the trunk lid.

"Sure. Let me just park." Derrick slipped back into the driver's seat and popped the gear shift into drive.

Under cover of the revving motor, Calen knocked on the trunk and listened as he walked behind the car. No answering knocks signaled him.

Derrick parked beside the office supply van. For good measure, Calen peered into the murky interior of that, too.

"Had to chaperone my girls on trick-or-treat tonight," Derrick said, his cowboy boots crunching gravel as he headed toward the building. He reached inside his black leather jacket, and Calen's heart performed an excited blip before Derrick's hand withdrew again, a litter of wrappered chocolate kisses on the palm. "Want one?"

"No, thanks."

Peeling foil off a candy, Derrick stepped inside the building, paused to switch on the light, and moved on. Calen, following, considered shouting for Maxey. But if she couldn't answer, he would have tipped off Derrick to what he suspected. He clamped his lips together and strained to hear in the quiet.

"Well, this sort of vindicates me," Derrick said, unwrapping a second candy as he walked to a door in the west wall. "You see this is open? It looks like the Hills are the ones who didn't batten down all the hatches tonight. This opens into their part of the building." He pushed it wider. "They left a light on in here, too. Avery?" He leaned through the opening.

"Do they usually leave the van here at night?" Calen asked.

He tried to envision what good it would do Derrick to take this little diversionary side trip. Because he was studying Derrick's back so closely, he saw it stiffen.

Derrick whirled around, his face ghost-white. "Dead," he choked out. "Blood."

Calen rushed him, shoved him hard into the wall beside the door and used the door frame to launch himself into the cramped little room. He had no thought of protecting his own back, no fear except of what he was about to see.

The first thing to register was the prevalence of red. A split second later what confused him was the unexpectedness of two. Two bloody people lay on the bloody floor. In spite of the awful damage to their heads, it was obvious. Calen drew a deep, painful breath.

Neither one was Maxey.

Scotty thumped down on one of the benches facing Fourteenth Street. Feet planted far apart, hands on knees, elbows akimbo, he bent toward the pavement to breathe. Hell of a thing, getting old.

He made himself sit there taming his lungs and heart to slow and steady. He wouldn't do Maxey any good in an intensive care unit.

The empty intersection added to the eeriness of the night and Scotty's present state of mind. Although not one car loomed in sight, he waited for the traffic light to switch to *Walk* before he rose and crossed the street. He plodded the last block with the steady determination of a turtle. No one seeing him would have noticed him gritting his teeth against irrationally breaking into a run again.

Reaching Fifteenth Street, he strained to see any activity halfway up the next block. No lights, no sirens. He changed course in the middle of the street, heading north, toward the entrance to the alley. In the distance from every direction, Boulder's canine population made itself known, stirred up by the begging denizens of the night.

Scotty checked his watch. Nine minutes since he'd left the office. There should be cops. Fists in pockets, he shrugged his denim jacket higher on his neck as he turned into the alley.

In the poor light, he thought he could make out four, unlit vehicles parked at about the futon store. As his legs marched him closer, the four resolved themselves into a panel van, a light-colored sedan, and two police cars.

Scotty ducked to look inside the latter—both empty—and kept moving toward the small door on the rear of the building. As he put out a hand to try it, the door swept outward and a long-haired guy in black leather trooped out, an Hispanic cop right on his tail.

The blond, his face as ghastly white as any mask Scotty had seen this night, didn't react to the close encounter. The cop took a side step away from Scotty, and his hand dipped automatically to the gun holster on his hip.

"Sir? I need you to stop right there and state your business."

Scotty held up both hands. "I'm the one who called 911. Scotty Springer."

The policeman didn't relax. "Would you step over to the patrol car please? That one. Wait right there."

Doing as he was told, trying to telepath his harmlessness, Scotty watched the cop shunt the other civilian—Derrick Sikes, was Scotty's confident bet—to the other police car and close him into the back seat.

Returning to Scotty, the cop appeared only slightly less wary of being jumped and disarmed. "Would you wait in the back of this car, Mr. Springer." The words were a question, but the inflection was declaratory.

"Wait for what?" Scotty crouched over to insert himself through the door the cop held for him. "What's happened?"

"We'll explain shortly, sir."

"Is Calen—Marshall Taylor—inside there?"

"I believe so." The cop stepped back to shut the door.

"Tell him I'm out here," Scotty shouted over the slam and glowered at the cop going into the building without a backward glance.

The two patrol cars sat nose to nose. Alley lamplight outlined the head of the man in the other one, giving him a pale aura as he twisted to look one way and then another out the windows.

Scotty laced his fingers and commanded himself not to fidget, but after five minutes of nothing happening, he sighed hard and tested the door handle. It was locked, of course.

He'd sat in the wrong half of patrol cars before, though not for anything more serious than an auto mishap to be sorted out. Under the current circumstances, he felt trapped and mistreated. For one thing, it smelled like a bus depot restroom in here.

At the same time he appreciated the policeman's caution in neutralizing him, a stranger, Scotty resented not being immediately recognized as an honest, innocent citizen who had a right to know what the hell was going on.

As he slouched deeper in the seat to put his head back for a nap, Calen came out of the building. Scotty rapped on the side window and waved.

A different cop—a woman with frizzy red hair erupting under her billed cap—followed the fire marshall out and nodded when he pointed at Scotty. In a moment, Calen had opened the car door, but before Scotty could duck out, Calen leaned over, hand on the roof, to confer.

"She's not here," he said.

Breathing deep of the crisp night air, Scotty settled back against the seat. The lady cop wandered over to the delivery van and shined her flashlight into the driver's side window. She looked as if she'd have a rich, hearty laugh, if there was ever a reason for it.

Scotty nodded at the other patrol car. "You think Sikes

knows where she is?"

"No, I don't. He and I arrived together. But the police will be taking him in for questioning. There are nearly a dozen gallon milk jugs inside his store, apparently all of them full of kerosene."

"So what are we waiting for?"

"Homicide. There're also two bodies inside. We don't have an identity yet, but it's probably the office supply owners—Mr. and Mrs. Hill."

Scotty squirmed and cussed. "You sure Maxey isn't in there, too?"

"Almost positive. We searched both sides of the building. Some kind of chase seems to have taken place in the Hills' half. Furniture is overturned, displays knocked down."

Scotty motioned Calen to get out of the way and spat through the open door as deftly as a baseball player.

A rolling Christmas tree of a fire truck, lit and silent, slipped into the east end of the alley, an ambulance tracking right behind. From the west end came an unmarked but equally official-looking black four-door automobile.

"They took their sweet time," Scotty growled, nodding at the firemen spilling out of the truck.

"I canceled that part of your 911 as soon as I saw the situation. Surprised they don't have something better to do tonight."

Calen stalked toward his colleagues and they met, grave-faced, in the middle of the alley.

Meanwhile, the policewoman and the guys from the black car— homicide, surely—put their heads together farther west. Before any of them should notice and cork him up again, Scotty swung his feet out of the car, eased out, snicked shut the door, and crossed arms and ankles as he leaned against it.

The two gray-suited homicide detectives peeled off and let themselves into the building. After a moment, the firemen scaled their idling truck and rumbled off. The ambulance attendants shut themselves in their cab and watched out the windshield, their faces flat with boredom. The policewoman assumed parade rest, guarding the back entrance to the scene.

Calen rejoined Scotty. "I'm going to hang around here a while—see if the police turn up any clues. What do you want to do?"

"Didn't I see a sign in this block, 'fortunes read'? We need to explore every avenue."

"At least we've got all the law in Boulder County helping us look for her now."

Scotty gestured with his chin. "How'd they die?"

"Heads bashed in. Crow bar on the floor looks pretty suspicious."

For a couple of seconds, Scotty felt thankful he hadn't run fast enough to join in Calen's discovery. Then the dull ache of anxiety for Maxey came seeping back. Rubbing the nape of his neck, he did a slow turn, looking at nothing in particular. For the first time he noticed the scattering of onlookers gathered in back yards, understandably hungry for crumbs of explanation.

"I'm going to walk over to Spruce," Scotty said. "Check out her house again. Talk to Ollie Kraig. Then I'll get the Bronco and recheck everywhere else."

He reached out to clasp Calen's shoulder. It was like touching a taut bow string just before the arrow whined away.

Scotty's half hour of forced inactivity had recharged his energy. He strode the alley, the street, hoping for that first glimpse of light in Maxey's windows. Concentrating on that, he was almost to the porch steps before he realized—before he came to a hard stop, shoe soles skidding on the leaves that coated the sidewalk, staring up the street.

A scramble of middle-aged kids streamed by him, their plastic costumes crackling, trick-or-treat bags swinging. As they pranced on down the block, Scotty turned one way, then the other, in slow double-check.

Nowhere along the curb was there a white Toyota with a MAXEY license plate.

12

Calen described the missing car to Sergeant Koebel. Her brown eyes glittered with intelligence as she relayed the information to the dispatcher on her hand set. Calen allowed hope to flirt around the edges of his worry. Maxey's car's disappearance didn't mean she was okay—how many times did cars and women meet foul play together?—but it gave the police something more tangible to search for.

He tried to smile reassurance at Scotty, who rocked from foot to foot while he squinted up and down the alley, obviously too wound up to feel the fatigue that sagged his face. The night was getting quieter and colder. The neighbors had all lost interest and dispersed.

"Scotty, give me the keys to the Bronco," Calen said. "I'll bring it back here and we'll cruise a bit."

"I'll go with you. We ought to look in at the office one more time." Scotty struck out west up the alley.

"Keep me informed," Calen said to Koebel.

"Sure thing," she raised her voice as he jogged to catch up with Scotty.

They stopped at the newspaper office first. Calen and Scotty stood in the middle of the room which had not changed in any detail since they stood there last. Their mood of frustration added to a sense of deja vu. The purple box and the arson device still lay on the table, and the matchbook, pink paper clip, and white barrette littered the floor where Calen had dropped them.

Outside, the deserted mall had lost its terrors. Tomorrow—a work day and school day—loomed larger. Scotty couldn't bear to think of the morning dawning, having to come to work, possibly alone.

"How do you figure it, her car gone like that?" he asked.

Calen shook his head. "Someone stole it."

Scotty thought someone had taken more than Maxey's Toyota. Calen probably thought so, too.

"She sure couldn't have driven it off herself," Calen said, his expression indicating his confusion as to whether this was good or bad news. "I've got her keys."

"She kept a spare key in a magnetic box in one of the wheel wells."

"She did? How'd you know that?" Calen snapped, as if this were some intimate secret he hadn't known about Maxey.

Scotty shrugged. "Too bad she doesn't have a car phone. We could call the number and see who answers."

"Let's go after my station wagon instead of the Bronco. We can listen to the police band radio while we drive."

They went out the back door, and Scotty wished to hell it was the last time tonight he'd have to fumble in the dark locking the damned thing.

"Scotty, you haven't known Maxey long. What—a little more than a year? And yet you probably know her better than anyone else does."

Not sure what Calen had in mind, Scotty marched without comment into the night along one more badly lit alley.

"To tell the truth," Calen went on, "I've been a little jealous of you. Your rapport with her."

Scotty hooted quietly. "You're the one with a key to her apartment. I'd call that pretty damn good rapport."

"Yeah." He didn't sound convinced.

A low, dark shape with red reflector eyes slunk across

the alley. Scotty hoped it wasn't a black cat.

Calen continued to think out loud. "A few nights ago I worked up the gumption to ask her to marry me. I did a lousy job of it. Before I even got all the words out, she said she wasn't interested in marriage. She wouldn't even commit to moving in with me at my house." Calen's low voice gave no indication of emotion lurking behind his words. "Then we had a couple of disputes about how she was going to protect herself. I wanted to be bodyguard, and she preferred a police whistle and a shot of tear gas.

"It kills me to admit it," he went on. "I'm a grown man, for God's sake. But she ticked me off enough that I stayed away and moped for the last couple of days. I should have met her after work tonight. At least been waiting for her at her place."

Scotty hated this kind of talk, hated being the wailing wall for a guilty conscience to bounce against. Still, he was good at it. He had the empathy for it. His own conscience wasn't all that clear.

"Son, your being there or not being there, tonight or tomorrow night or a week from Wednesday, makes no difference. You couldn't be watching her all the time. She wouldn't allow it."

Calen gave a quick, mirthless laugh. "You've got that right. You know what a prickly porcupine she is whenever she thinks someone's encroaching on her independence. She thinks she can take care of herself. She insists on it." He drew a long, shuddering breath. "That's just Maxey. I love her for it."

Seemingly embarrassed at the admission, he picked up the pace as they emerged on Eleventh Street and bent into the climb north toward Pine. There were no longer any barricades or red-vested men preventing vehicles from cruising down to Pearl Street. The houses here glowed with mellow lights deep inside or upstairs. The occupants, winding down the day, would be performing the rituals that led to sleep. An occasional jack-o'-lantern flickered forgotten on a porch.

Scotty spotted the white station wagon ahead and across the street, under a street lamp that stuttered and buzzed. He felt exactly like that light—inefficient and burning out way too fast.

Maxey drove the Toyota as if it were a tank made of glass. She gripped the steering wheel with both fists so hard they throbbed, her stiff foot tentative on the gas pedal. As she lumbered along Iris, westbound, everyone else zipped past in fast forward.

She couldn't remember getting from Spruce Street to here, couldn't understand why she *was* here or think where she would go next. All her wits focused on the unchangeable past, when her taped wrists had forced her hands into an attitude of prayer. She lived again her anger and fear, Mrs. Hill coming at her with the pungent cloth, the unholy feel of her splayed fingers jabbing into Mr. Hill's eyes, the wet thump of metal against flesh and bone, the blood that all the perfumes of Arabia could never. . . her anger and fear, Mrs Hill coming at her. . . .

Calen took the streets at random, Pine to Broadway, south then east. Neither he or Scotty said much. The police band now and then burst into sporadic activity, none of it relevant to the murders or Maxey's APB. Once they hung a hard U-turn to catch up to a white Toyota, but the license plate was Mississippi.

"Let's swing by the Underwood house again," Calen said. "The villain is always the least likely suspect, and right now, in my book, B. J. is it."

The dark shape beside Maxey kept shifting and squirming, rustling, tapping, humming.

"Well." His sudden voice convulsed her hands on the steering wheel, and the car gave a sickening little lurch into the oncoming lane. A horn Dopplered angrily as she overcorrected the other way.

"I guess you're thankful I arrived in the nick of time," he said. "You'd be dead right now if I hadn't." He flounced on the seat, and his cloak huffed a musty sigh. "I'm your hero."

There was no room in Maxey's aching head for gratitude. "You've been following me," she said dully.

"Lucky for you, huh?" His feet beat a constant tattoo against the floor mat. "I've got to admit, I started shadowing you because I was mad at you and I wanted to scare you. But, hey, when the time came, I just had to rescue you. What a great feeling. What a kick!"

"You didn't need to kill them." For a moment, her vision blurred and another horn yelled at her.

He didn't seem to notice her spastic driving. "You looked so funny, walking across the street with a big frog. It's a good thing you screamed, later, you know, in the store. Or I wouldn't have realized you needed me. I let myself in the building right away—didn't hesitate at all—but then I played it smart. I snuck around and hid behind shelves and stuff till I got an idea of what was going down. I was a regular James Bond."

"You didn't have to kill them."

He bounced on the seat again, reached up and ripped off the pirate scarf. His hair crackled with static electricity. "I bet you were astonished to see me come roaring in. I'd had my eye on that pry bar, and I whipped it up and wham! Down goes the old lady. And bam, the old man gets it right in the kisser." He brushed at his black sleeve. "Good thing I wore something doesn't show stains."

"You didn't have to kill them!"

"*They* were going to kill *you*!"

She bit her upper lip and concentrated on coming to a complete stop at a red light in front of Community Hospital.

"I may have a slight concussion," she said. "How about letting me out here? You can have the car."

"Gee, thanks, Maxey. Thing is, I don't have a valid driver's license any more. I lost my license a few years ago.

When I was incarcerated for stealing a car."

She felt him turning to look at her to catch her reaction to this. She stared stony-faced straight ahead.

"I never bothered to renew my license since I couldn't afford an automobile anyway, what with the insurance and gasoline and all. I always walk or take a bus. Okay, green light." He fluttered one hand, shooing her on. "As soon as we can, we'll get you to a doctor. After we collect my poetry."

"If you don't have a car, how did you follow me to Calen's—Table Mesa—and fool around with my laundry?"

His laugh was delighted. "I splurged for a cab. Boy, that was a kick, too. More James Bond. 'Follow that white car.' And then—am I creative or am I creative? The mystery of the wandering laundry. I wish I could have seen your face."

"Did you really have a knife that night in my backyard?"

He lightly punched her shoulder. "That's for me to know and you to find out, missy."

There was no question he was armed now. Just before he pushed and pulled Maxey out of the office supply building and over to Spruce Street and her car, he'd shown her the pistol he wrested out of Avery Hill's bloody pants pocket.

"Turn here," Robert ordered. "Shortcut to the Bluebell parking lot."

"I can't just drop you off at your home. We need to go to the police." Maxey completed the turn, but she pulled in next to the curb of the dark, narrow street. "I showed you where my spare car key was so we could drive to the police!"

"We will go to the police. It's on the list. Poems, doctor, police. Busy night, huh?"

"What have your damned poems got to do with it?"

"Maxey." He drew out the name reproachfully. "Profanity is not—not—ladylike. So anyway, you'll want my poetry for a sidebar to the story you're going to write about me for this week's paper. 'Roberto Trueblood, local poet, is hero in daring rescue of newspaper editor on Halloween night.' I have to get my writing pad, too. I've got all these ideas and feelings just bursting to be poems. I can write while we're at the police station waiting for the photographers and reporters."

He put his hand on her wrist and she shook it off as if it burned.

"Don't worry, Maxey. I'll talk to your competitors from the *Camera* and the *Post* or wherever, but I'll save back the best quotes for you and the *Regard*."

Maxey lowered her head to rest on her hands strangling the steering wheel.

"Come on, what are we sitting here for?" Robert demanded. "My public awaits."

She straightened up and eased her foot off the brake.

"There's an entrance at the end of this block," he directed. "See it? Left. *Left*. Whoops. That's okay. Everyone drives over that curb. Park anywhere."

She braked immediately, crosswise to the few other cars in the Bluebell lot.

When she didn't move to improve their position, Robert said, "Good," and stretched to shut off the engine and take out the key. He opened his door and bounded out. Looking back in at Maxey, he said, "Come on."

"I'll wait here."

"No. You have to come with me. It's dangerous out here for you, alone in the dark."

Maxey laughed. It might have developed into a full-scale fit of hysteria, but her head hurt worse with the exertion.

"Robert, you don't want me to come inside with you. I'm seriously considering throwing up."

"No problem. It happens all the time in there."

Maxey stared up at the building, at the dull stone lit by weak floodlights and watery pools of windows. It loomed like an inside-out cave.

She clenched her jaw. "No, Robert. I'll wait for you

here."

"No, Maxey, you'll come in. Dang it, I hate stubborn women." He slapped the car roof to vent his irritation. "You'd better take me seriously, Maxey. The last snippy woman who insisted on having her own way—I almost killed her."

He tilted his face to the sky and painstakingly counted aloud to ten. "Eleven and twelve, for good measure." He twisted back to smile at Maxey. "Hey, I didn't 'almost' anything tonight. I did kill a couple of people. I don't think you have any choice but to do what I say. Do you?" He dug enthusiastically into the depths of the cloak to produce Avery Hill's gun. Flourishing it at Maxey, he dropped into the passenger seat again.

"We can patrol twice as much territory if we split up," Calen said. "Let's go get your Bronco. You can take everything north of Pearl Street and I'll cover everything south."

But later, idling past his own dark house, Calen missed having Scotty beside him, sharing his unspoken misery.

On an impulse, he grabbed the phone from under the dash and dialed the public safety building to ask for Emilio Madrid, who probably wouldn't be on duty. But he was, and he was even at home base.

"What can I do for you, Marshall Taylor?" his soft, Spanish-tinged voice came through the receiver.

"You may have heard that Maxey Burnell is missing."

"Yes. Bad news."

"When you were checking on B.J. Underwood and Robert Truet, did you run a check on prior offenses?"

"I did. Nothing turned up worth much. Nothing at all on Underwood. Truet was arrested ten years ago for car theft."

"Oh man, why didn't you tell me?"

"You see some connection between a guy stealing wheels and a stalker scaring Ms. Burnell?"

"Yeah, okay, you're right. It probably has no bearing.

That's all you found?"

"All that he got caught on."

Maxey rolled her head against the head rest of her seat, eyes shut, listening to Robert rant. She should have gone to his room without an argument and spared herself. Obviously he hadn't talked about this for a long time—it had logjammed in his mind, waiting for the right moment to spew forth.

"My buddy Larry and I stole this jewelry, see. Worth thousands—heck, millions, maybe. Bet you never met a robber-poet before, huh? Right now, I could be living in the Boulderado Hotel instead of the Bluebell House. But this woman from Chicago found out we had the stuff soldered inside our hubcaps, and so Larry made a run for it without me, and I never heard from him or the jewelry again, and I tried to murder the nosy sow, excuse my language, and failed, and so did she, fail I mean, because the police didn't arrest me for menacing or attempted murder or anything, for insufficient evidence, they just had sufficient evidence for auto theft—the Jeep I stole to go up in the mountains where she was. So don't start with me, missy."

She hoped she'd be able to laugh about this some day. "You win, Robert." She opened her door and had to make a conscious effort to lift both feet over the sill.

Robert came around to help her, both of his hands empty, the gun hiding in his clothes again. He ushered her to the double doors and into the building, then danced up the stairs ahead of her, his black cloak flapping like Poe's raven. Clumping after him, Maxey gripped the hand rail, which wobbled and squealed.

The first floor was surprisingly quiet for midnight and Halloween. The hall lay peaceful except for dueling televisions from three adjacent neighbors.

Robert galloped to the next stairway, stripping off the cloak and flinging it around like an inept matador. When he'd rushed halfway up the steps, Maxey reached the bottom one, and she hugged the unpleasantly sticky newel post, dizzy with effort.

"I'll wait here," she mumbled.

Peering back down at her, Robert rolled his eyes. He hip-hopped down to grasp and haul her up by one armpit.

At the top, she ripped herself free and weaved down the smoke-hazy hall after him. He produced a key, aimed it at the door knob, and leaned over for a closer inspection. Gingerly, he touched the splintered door frame.

"Damn kids. Fourth time this month they've busted in. Gonna put a sign on the door: no radio inside; no TV; no booze; no drugs; but, hey, help yourself to a poem." He pushed wide the door. "Look at this—they didn't even have the courtesy to shut off the light when they left."

He bowed low to Maxey. She crossed into the room, being careful not to touch him. Leaving the door open, Robert rushed from couch to table to bed, collecting papers and pads and pens.

Somewhere a door slammed, and someone came coughing along the hall. A tall man in a long gray coat strode past without looking in.

Dripping loose papers from the pile clutched to his chest, Robert called out, "Hey, Pendorf. Guess what."

The footsteps stopped and then returned. The tall man had an Indiana Jones hat, Prince Valiant hair, and eyes as blank as Frankenstein's monster. He gazed in at them, mouth slack with puzzlement.

Robert chortled. "You're going to read about me in the papers. I'm a certified hero. I saved this lady's life tonight."

Pendorf licked his rubbery lips. "You shittin' me, man?"

"Word of honor!" Robert tried to cross his heart and spilled more papers. He swooped to pick them up. "Tell him, Maxey."

Pendorf eyed her, his pupils round and dark as olives. "Bitchin' costume, girlfriend."

She looked down at herself, at the spray of blood stains on her sneakers, her jeans, her shirt—undoubtedly on her face and in her hair.

Since Robert was unconcerned about her being sick, she would vomit right here and now in the middle of his floor, or, even better, over there in the middle of his bed.

She didn't though. A lifetime of conditioning to be polite and in control helped her tamp down the reflex. She glowered at Pendorf till he swayed, turned, and shuffled on his way.

"Pendorf's vocabulary needs some Lysol, but he's an okay guy otherwise." Robert found a brown grocery sack and dumped his paperwork into it. "Okay. Ready. The way I see it—" He shrugged into the cloak again and crowded Maxey out the door and slammed it. "I see it as a column. Five or six poems every week. Does that sound like enough? I can do more."

"Robert—"

He hit the stairs and banged down them as if he were falling, waiting at the bottom for her to catch up.

"One thing, though," he said, striding ahead again. "I have to have the opportunity to proofread my stuff before it comes out. No offense, Maxey, but I've noticed typos in the *Regard* sometimes. I don't want any careless little errors creeping in to ruin the rhythm or the rhyme. Or the meaning. The mood. You know?"

"Robert—"

She followed him down the last of the stairs. He burst through the double doors to the parking lot, then held one open for her. The chill night air hit her face like a splash of cold water. He spun and trotted off. She dodged the closing door.

"Robert!"

He stopped and looked over his shoulder, his eyebrows hidden in the blind of his untidy bangs.

"All right, Robert, you win. I'll publish your poems. You are a poet. Your job is to write poetry."

He preened, rolling his shoulders in the cloak, his grin shy with satisfaction.

"But, Robert, you have to let me do my job, too. I'm an editor. When you turn in your work, it's up to me to make it fit my publication's guidelines."

In the sickly light from a wire-caged fixture above the door, Robert's mouth slid shut across his sepia teeth.

"Fit?" he said uncertainly.

"Right." Maxey risked nodding her head, her voice stronger as inspiration took hold. "I may have to cut words or add words to make your poem fit the space I have for it. And then, of course, there will be times I'll see ways to improve what you've done. I'll punch it up. Take out a dull phrase and insert a snappy one. You know."

"No, I don't know!" He actually stamped his foot. "When I finish a poem, it's exactly the way I want it."

Having found that her head would nod without dropping off, she tried shaking it, with equally gratifying results. "A professional writer isn't afraid to let a professional editor make professional changes. If you're so enamored of your own words, you're too conceited to write well."

She literally held her breath, afraid she had gone too far. The specter of a woman from Chicago who had won but yet failed with Robert, both encouraged and unnerved Maxey.

Hugging the sack of poetry between chest and crossed arms, Robert stared at her with all the horror he hadn't spared the Hills.

Scotty pulled into the Conoco station on North Twenty-Eighth Street for gas. He hooked the hose into the tank and heard his cell phone ring. Opening the door and bending in to answer it, he felt an emotional cocktail of hope and dread.

Calen's no-nonsense voice jumped into his ear. "She's at the police station."

Scotty squeezed his eyes closed, blinked them open.

"She's giving homicide a statement," Calen was saying.

"I'll be there in a few minutes." Scotty snapped shut the phone and backed out of the Bronco to disconnect the fuel pump with a quarter of a tank full.

While he bulled his way into southbound traffic, the phone chirped again.

"Are you coming to the police station?" Calen asked.

"Yes, damn it. Give me five minutes."

"Meet her in the lobby. She wants you to take her to the hospital."

"What's wrong with her? Calen? Calen?" He tossed the phone aside and braked for a red light. He'd worried about Maxey all evening, he could stand to worry about her for five minutes more.

It was five and a half minutes. He pulled up to the station on Thirty-Third Street and parked smack in front in a yellow zone, confident his errand qualified him for that.

Before he could unlatch his seat belt, Maxey came out of the building, swung open the passenger door and eased inside. Her face and hair looked as if she'd recently stuck them under a faucet—ruddy and wet-mussed, respectively. She had on Calen's brown leather jacket.

"Is Calen coming?" Scotty asked brusquely instead of grabbing and hugging the daylights out of her.

"He's filling out a report. He'll check on us later."

Scotty fired up the engine and swept a backward arc that pointed them to the exit. "We're going to the hospital?"

"Please. I got hit on the head. I don't think it's anything much, but it's better to be safe than to skip the X-ray and go to sleep and never wake up again and be really, really sorry." She leaned her head against the side window. "Oh, Scotty, what a horrible night. You know about Mr. and Mrs. Hill?"

"I know they're dead."

"They waylaid me and meant to kill me, because they thought I thought Sylvia thought they were trying to torch their business."

"Thought so." Scotty's breathing settled down closer to normal. "So who killed them?"

"Truet the poet. He thinks everyone's going to be thrilled

and amazed. Give him a front full of medals. Idiot."

They rode a while, not speaking, Boulder's night lights shimmering like jewels, the side streets deep and mysterious.

Finally Scotty couldn't help asking, "Why don't you want to marry Calen?"

She sat up the better to squint at him. "Why don't *you* want to marry him? Or more to the point, why doesn't he want to marry me?"

"He does want to marry you. Idiot."

The car was full of silence for a full half minute before he was relieved to hear her chuckle.

"I can't believe it. He wants to marry me? I wish you could hear how he asked me, Scotty. I'm so used to guys who won't or can't commit—my ex, the cop that I dated for a year, my dad. *You*, for goshsake. So I didn't even recognize a marriage opportunity when it's more or less—mostly less—offered." She sighed with exasperation—or maybe, Scotty hoped, with satisfaction.

After a beat, she said, "I'm never going to find out who Sylvia was. How could I expect to understand her when I don't even know who *I* am? I almost murdered two people tonight. I almost murdered two people." She shrank into the oversized jacket, and her voice skidded toward tears. "If Robert Truet hadn't come along and done it for me, I would have used that crow bar on those old people myself."

"Self defense," Scotty murmured.

"I've got to get a grip on my life. Sylvia can rest in peace. Ditto Basil. Whatever B. J. Underwood is up to, I don't want to know."

Scotty opened his mouth and snapped it shut again as she went on talking.

"No more investigative reporting. I'm going to do ads and public service messages. Entertainment. Weather. Sports."

They'd hit every red light on the way across town. Here was the last one, with the hospital hunkering just across the intersection.

"What happened to Robert?" Scotty asked.

"I promised to publish his poems, but I also threatened to edit them. It freaked him out so bad, he let me drive to the police station and turn him in. Actually, he was preoccupied at the time, composing a poem about the sanctity of a creative writer's own words."

"He'll have loads more inspiration for poetry in jail."

"Oh, yeah, to say nothing of being a big hero and getting a ticker tape parade." Maxey's mouth twisted, as if the sarcasm tasted bitter. "Jerk," she muttered.

Scotty angled up the side street and drove under the emergency entrance canopy.

"Wait a minute. I'll come around," he said, but of course she already had the door open and her feet on the pavement by the time he got there.

He thought she hadn't noticed the white station wagon that followed them the last few blocks and now parked at the street curb. But she was definitely trying to smile as she let Scotty take her elbow and guide her to the spotlighted glass door.

The short walk felt like some kind of stupid contest to see which of them could shake the most.

She hated hospitals. The last time she was flat on her back in a hospital, a lover had told her good-bye. This time, this one was telling her hello. Her hand gripped Calen's hand hard enough to cut off circulation to both.

The doctor on call had gone to arrange Maxey's admittance for overnight observation. She didn't have the energy to argue against it, which probably meant she needed to be here.

"All undressed and nowhere to go," she joked.

The emergency room's high bed felt as hard as a table, which reminded her of the Hill's office table, which made her twitch and moan.

"Hey. You okay?" Calen leaned toward her from the straight chair he'd pulled up beside her hip.

"Just having a wicked flashback."

The doctor—a small man with a large nose and a gaudy geometric tie flopping free of his white lab jacket—came bustling back. "We'll have a room for you in about half an hour."

"Thanks, Dr.—" Maxey squinted at his name tag. "—Rudderly." The name sounded familiar.

"Do you need anything for pain?" he asked, hands on hips, staring so hard at her, she thought she must look even worse than she felt.

The decision was too much for her. She wanted to fall asleep and wake up a week from now in her own bed.

"I know who you are," she mumbled. "You were Sylvia Wellman's physician when she came to ER."

He frowned, not recognizing the name.

For perhaps ten seconds, Maxey felt the old burning need-to-know, the familiar questioning curiosity that preceded a good interview. Then she remembered her vow to Scotty in the car, to stick to sports and weather. She just didn't care anymore about the real mysteries of life. Rudderly might have talked to Sylvia long enough to know exactly who she was and why, but Maxey just didn't care anymore.

"Give her something for pain," Calen said. "She's too stubborn to ask for it."

The doctor left, patting Maxey's ankle as he went, and the gesture, which she'd usually have considered condescending, felt nurturing all out of proportion to its importance.

She sniffed and glared at the acoustical ceiling tiles, yellowed with age. Calen laced his fingers with hers. Beyond the curtained cubicle, the hospital hummed and murmured and carried on with business.

Turning her head to look full at Calen, Maxey said, "Talk to me."

"What about?"

"Whatever's on your mind."

"That's easy." He sucked in a deep breath. "I love you, Maxey. Move in with me. Hell, marry me, if you want."

It might not be William Shakespeare, but it was close enough.

13

From the November 17th issue of the *Blatant Regard*:

Twenty-five-year-old Robert Truet, alias Roberto Trueblood, remains in custody at the Boulder County jail with bond set at $150,000, accused of the bludgeon slaying of Avery and Hester Hill, the owners of Hill's Office Supply. His public defender, Fayette Lanker, says his defense will be based on Truet's intent to protect a fourth person, Maxey Burnell, whom the Hills had kidnapped and threatened to kill. Truet, a longtime resident of the Bluebell House, is not worried about the outcome, and he does not complain about his confinement. A poet, he spends his time writing such thoughts as Serenity, *which follows here, in its entirety.*

"Ne'r call ME 'coward' nor 'shirker,'

For I glimpsed the jibbering [sic] countenance of not one but two Grim Reapers,

And I grinned and went on the bold and bloody offensive,

That ended with ME the absolutely victorious."

From the same issue of the *Regard:*

The Boulder division of International Business Machines is pleased to announce the recent acquisition of U. S. patents by four employees. The four men, who will receive gold fountain pens from IBM as well as checks for their efforts, are T. Steffen Kerr, Alonzo Dal, B.J. Underwood. . . .

From the same issue of the *Regard:*

For sale: Used furniture. Dinette table w/four chairs. Dbl bed w/oak bookcase headboard, matching bureau. Couch and asst upholstered chairs—good condtn excpt minor cat scrtchs. Must sell. Owner moving. Make offer. Contact Regard *for more information and appt to see. Phone 303-447-5. . . .*

From the December 15th issue of the *Regard:*

STROLLIN' THE PEARL with Maxey

****Derrick Sikes will soon be announcing the grand opening of A Lode Of Furniture, formerly The Futon Lode, newly remodeled and expanded to twice its former capacity. Derrick's slogan will be "Come in and take a load off." Whether his hours of planning and carpentering will pay off remains to be seen, but they haven't hurt his love life. He and wife Torry are expecting their third little chest and drawers in March.*

Morrie Lutz, the ever-eupeptic proprietor of the Dilly Delicatessen, has added a new item to the menu board—a meat hater's sandwich to live for. Called the Veggiemanic, it begins with a fresh sourdough bun and two or three kinds of cheese, not just melted but toasted *to a chewy, gorgeous gold. On top of that come sliced red tomatoes, a handful of crispy bean sprouts, a dusting of chopped mushrooms, and a layer of raw carrot/cauliflower/ broccoli confetti. The paper-thin sweet Bermuda onion rings are optional. Kids, don't try this at home! You'd never quite get Morrie's spin on this splendiferous grub.*

Tis the Christmas season, but at The Jug and Lantern, owner Mick O'Fallon is feeling more like Halloween. According to Mick, his restaurant, which does dispense some lively spirits, seems lately to be haunted by one. The symptoms are a cabinet door refusing to stay shut, matchbooks and menus suddenly falling off shelves, pens and whole boxes of paper clips disappearing. Mick even has a name for his not unfriendly ghost—Packy.

Packy was the nickname of Sylvia Wellman, a local figure who died of pneumonia, following a bad fall on a flight of stairs, in October. Not much was known about Sylvia, a loner who regularly cruised Pearl Street collecting freebies from the merchants. She was born in 1930 in Hagerstown, Indiana, the older of identical twins. Her sister, Margretta, died in a school bus accident when the girls were eight years old. Sylvia never married. At one time she worked as secretary to a congressman in the South Dakota state legislature. She came to Boulder in the late 1960's, but why, or where she lived and worked, is unknown.

And here's something to marvel about. Research in the field of twin bereavement indicates that a lone twin always feels incomplete and forever misses the sibling even if that sibling was stillborn.

What do you think? Maybe Margretta had something to do with Sylvia being Packy.

Then again, maybe Sylvia just liked paper clips and rubber bands. Hey, everybody needs a hobby.

Who is the author of WHO WAS SYLVIA??

Carol Cail grew up in southwestern Ohio, taught eighth grade history in Fayetteville, Arkansas, gave birth to two sons in Lexington, Kentucky, and now resides north of Denver with her amicable husband and an antisocial cat.

Her six previously published novels include three Maxey Burnell mysteries. Her short stories have appeared in mystery and horror magazines, and in several anthologies. She's also a poet, a book reviewer, and a lecturer on how to write. She feels she's at the perfect age to give advice: old enough to have had plenty of experiences, and young enough to remember what they are.

Away from the computer, Carol enjoys cooking, hates house-cleaning, is proud of her two grandchildren, and cherishes being married to the same man for forty-three years, who just sold their office supply store and is safe and sound in retirement.

"Please watch for my next Deadly Alibi mystery, THE SEEDS OF TIME," Carol says. "And remember, anyone can have an out-of-body experience. It's called reading."

Printed in the United States
16308LVS00001B/170